Ritwik Ghatak
stories

Translated from Bengali by

Rani Ray

THORNBIRD
NIYOGI BOOKS

Published by
NIYOGI BOOKS
Block D, Building No. 77,
Okhla Industrial Area, Phase-I,
New Delhi-110 020, INDIA
Tel: 91-11-26816301, 26818960
Email: niyogibooks@gmail.com
Website: www.niyogibooksindia.com

Design: Nabanita Das

ISBN: 978-93-86906-43-4
Publication: 2018

Printed at: Niyogi Offset Pvt. Ltd., New Delhi, India

Contents

In Lieu of an

Introduction

I

For film lovers, whether in India or abroad, Ritwik Ghatak surely needs no introduction. But his short stories are less known than his films. For readers, therefore, a few words may be necessary by way of an introduction.

Some artists and writers, after having reached the top, appear to long for a 'second love'—a medium which is different from that in which they had established their reputation. The insatiable urge for challenges and adventures on a new soil of productivity probably drove Rabindranath Tagore to seriously take up painting in his late sixties. Or, was it a sense of impatience with the available tools of expression in poetry, which he felt were inadequate for communicating the new and complex concerns that were agonizing him in the 1930s? Were Satyajit Ray's forays into the domain of science fiction and detective stories mere exercises in leisurely relaxation, or did they imply something deeper - a multidimensional artist's restless search for the right media form that would suitably express a particular idea or mood of his?

Unlike Tagore's paintings or Ray's fiction, the bulk of the stories that make up this volume are not experiments by a famous artist in search of a 'second love.' They were written by an individual long before he became famous as a powerful personality in another artistic field - the films. They belong to a phase in his life which could be described as that of his 'first love' - when as a young imaginative artist, he was groping for a medium that would best suit his creative urges. Like many other artists who spend their initial years of apprenticeship in stumbling from one area to another, experimenting with a variety of media, and finally discovering the most suitable one for their artistic creativity, Ritwik Ghatak also traversed this entire complex artistic terrain before he could reach the medium with which he could find himself in rapport - although he was never totally satisfied.[1]

Ritwik's short stories were an outcome of a brief sojourn during this intellectual odyssey of his. As can be seen, most of the stories in this volume were written within a short span of three or four years, between 1947 and 1950. In order to understand them, therefore, we may have to reverse our gears - from the present to the past, from our familiarity with Ritwik, the famous film-maker of the 1950–70 period, to our search for a young and unknown writer, struggling to shape his own voice during those tumultuous years of a post-War Bengal - lacerated

1. Cf. "The cinema can mould minds of millions at a single time in a complete way. I came to cinema because of that... if tomorrow there evolves a better medium than cinema, I'll kick our cinema (and opt for the other). I don't love film." -Ritwik Ghatak's interview in 1973, reprinted in *Chitrabikshan*, January-April, 1976. P.65.

by communal riots and the 1947 Partition - and ending up in the pathetic hopelessness of the post-Independence era.

Is a reading of Ritwik's stories then merely a nostalgic exercise in remembering a past? Is this collection simply a personal tribute by a handful of his contemporaries and admirers-just to remind his audience of another facet of his versatility which was eclipsed by the more obvious wealth and virtuosity of his later filmography?

It is certainly beyond all this. We strongly feel that these stories are not to be celebrated as mere museum-pieces in a *Ritwikiana,* but need to be recognized historically as the first artistic steps that led to Ritwik's entry into the portals of cinematography. They therefore claim to be very much a living part of the on-going research on Ritwik Ghatak's films. They are as essential as his films, for an understanding of the totality of his being that went to the making of those films. Critics and students have so far depended mainly on his scattered articles, snatches of reminiscences and stray observations, for supplementing their own appreciation of Ritwik's films. The present collection may yield to them—both in India and abroad—another major source, albeit indirect, that can help them to explore some of the hidden or less-known origins that might have shaped Ritwik's filmography.

At the same time, those who want to read these stories for their own sake, as self-contained literary pieces-without any obligation to discover in them embryonic signs of Ritwik's future films—are at liberty to interpret the various layers of meanings that they yield. They are works of miniaturist art in their own right—and as deftly-crafted short stories, some of them can easily rival the best in this genre.

II

Ritwik Kumar Ghatak was born on November 4, 1925 in Dhaka (now in Bangladesh). He was the youngest (along with his twin sister) of nine children of a senior government official who, in the course of his assignments, was posted in different parts of the then undivided Bengal. Ritwik thus grew up in surroundings which provided him with the rich and unforgettable experience of traditional rural life in eastern Bengal. At the same time, he received abundant intellectual stimuli from his family environs that were home to modern European ideas and literature. These two basic ingredients of tradition and modernity shaped Ritwik's artistic temperament.

Remembering his childhood, spent mostly in the small towns of east Bengal in the pre-Partition era, Ritwik was to write later: "My days were spent on the banks of the Padma—the days of an unruly and wild child. The people on the passenger boats looked like dwellers of some distant planet. The large merchant ships coming from Patna, Bankipore, Monghyr, carried sailors speaking a strange tongue, in a mixture of broken rural Hindi and the dialect of those from across the Padma. I saw the fishermen. In the drizzling rain of the village they would, in sudden joy, break into some mad tune which would pull at your heartstrings with the sudden gusts of wind and make you yearn for something vague...." Once in autumn, he sailed off on a boat and lost his way among tall grasses where snakes hid. Overwhelmed with the pollens of the grass, he almost got choked. but the memory of the pollens remained with him forever. At another time, he got hired to act in a play, missed his train, and landed up in a remote village at nightfall. It was the night before the full moon. In front of him was a haunted lake. He punted down the lake with a friend in the gathering darkness.[2]

One can find in these memories of sensuous experiences, the raw materials with which Ritwik was to build up the environs in his short stories, and later composed the unforgettable visuals and music of his films. The call of the wild and the unknown also made the child Ritwik run away from home a few times. This childhood search for an El Dorado was to become a metaphor for the adventures of a truant little boy who lands up, in the course of his search in a metropolis, in the film *Bari Thekey Paliye,* which he made in 1959. The El Dorado turns out to be an arena of fierce struggle for existence. But years before he made the film, Ritwik quite often went back to the theme of El Dorado in several of his short stories where he dealt with the fragile base of the El Dorado which collapses once we try to shift it from one place to another, or from one time frame to a different one. *Akashgangar Srot Dhorey* (On the Trail of the Milky Way) and *Ecstasy* are two representative examples, where he talks about the incompatibility between the dream and the stark reality.

By the time he was seventeen years old, Ritwik's wanderings had yielded to him a rich harvest of experiences. In the course of one of his escapades in the early 1940s, he had a stint as an employee in the bill department of a textile mill in Kanpur. It helped him to gain insight into working class life—an understanding which stood him in good stead when he wrote stories against the backdrop of trade union struggles, like *Chokh (Eyes) and Comrade.*

---

2. *Chhabi Kara* (Making Films) published first in *Amrita,* Sports and Entertainment Special Issue, 1969, and reprinted in *Chitrabikshan,* op.cit.

Besides this treasure trove of colourful experiences that Ritwik acquired during his rovings as an adolescent, the other source of his artistic inspiration was the intellectual ambience of his domestic surroundings. His father, Suresh Kumar Ghatak, a bureaucrat of the colonial administration, was trained and steeped in Western cultural values and norms. But like many other Indian bureaucrats of his generation, he retained and nurtured his traditional cultural roots while accepting and adopting the ideas offered by the West. He was a scholar of Sanskrit. From him, Ritwik was believed to have imbibed his love for the ancient Hindu scriptures and Indian Classical literature—references to which abound in his films, as well as the short stories.

Ritwik's eldest brother Manish Ghatak—who was 23 years older than him—had already earned fame as a writer of fiction when Ritwik was growing up. Writing under the *nom de plume* of *Yuvanashva,* he was one of the pioneers of the *Kallol* group of writers. They sought to introduce in Bengali fiction a style of Naturalism of sorts—*a la Zola*—and were influenced by later writers like Knut Hamsun and Freud. However extraneous the stylistic source of their writings might have been, we have to admit that the Kallol writers were the first to make bold attempts to explore the life-style of the Bengali lower orders (e.g. the urban slum-dwellers, the coal-mine workers, the criminals from the underworld), or the complex psyche of the marginalized middle class citizen of a metropolis. They tried to describe all these facets in the raw. The influence of Manish Ghatak and the *Kallol* group on Ritwik's artistic development cannot be totally ignored. Ritwik's story *Raja,* which cynically describes the adventure of a Bengali middle class bounder turned pick-pocket, harks back in a certain sense to the *Kallol* spirit.

Another brother of Ritwik's, Sudhish Ghatak, was trained as a documentary cameraman in the UK, and in the late 1930s worked with the then well-known New Theatres company in India in the making of several feature films. Thus, even when young Ritwik was groping among the prevalent conventional media for avenues to express his talents, at the back of his mind the medium of film as an alternative must have also been emerging as a possibility.

From his childhood, therefore, Ritwik's mind was opened up to a variety of cultural influences. His earliest attempts to give shape to these various streams of impressions and ideas were in the field of poetry. But he soon realized that he was not made for it. He recalled those days in a humorous vein in his later life: "As usual with Bengali boys—and I believe it's the same with the French—whenever the creative urge comes up within them for the first time, it breaks out into poetry. So, my artistic activities also began with a few badly written poems. Then I realized that it was not my cup of tea. I knew that I would never be able to enter even the fringes of a hundred-thousand mile stretch around 'poesy'!"[3]

In the meantime, Ritwik was veering towards politics. The 1940s, the decade when Ritwik was growing up from adolescence to youth, were a tumultuous period in the history of India. Events were moving at a rapid pace. The outbreak of the Second World War was followed by the anti-Fascist movement launched by the Communists and progressive intellectuals. The 1943 famine in Bengal that wiped out millions, exposed the ruthlessness of the economic policies of the

3. *Chitrabikshan*, op.cit. p.64.

British colonial order. Waves of anti-imperialist outbursts surged up in the 1942 'Quit India' agitation, the wide-spread working class struggles and militant peasant movements in the post-War period, the mutiny in the navy in 1946, and the military activities of the INA. Although the Indian Communists mistakenly adopted a hostile attitude towards the 1942 movement and the INA, they played an active role in the 1943 famine relief operations, led the famous *Tebhaga* struggle of the share-croppers in rural Bengal, and workers' strikes in the industrial areas, and fought the British in the RJN mutiny. They could therefore establish themselves as a major force in the social and political scene of Bengal in those days. Recalling those events, Ritwik later described his own feelings and attitudes in an interesting interview: "By then I had been drawn towards Marxist politics. It was not a mere leaning. I was an activist. Although I was not a card-holder (of the Party), I was a close sympathizer, a fellow-traveller of sorts."[4]

It was during this water-shed in his life, that Ritwik turned to short stories. In his own words: "I began to write stories from then onwards. But the urge to write stories was not like those earlier vapid and hollow attempts at composing poetry. (In my new phase as a short story writer) Even at that early age, it was the desire as a political being to protest vehemently against the wickedness, the villainy, the oppression that I saw around me, which drove me to write short stories."[5]

That he took it up as a serious business was evident from the fact that at that time, when he was an undergraduate student in

---

4. Ibid.

5. Ibid. pp. 64-65

Rajshahi in east Bengal, he founded and edited a magazine called *Abhidhara*, "closely set on Marxist lines." It ran for a few months, and had to close down due to the inevitable lack of funds. Some of his stories were published in this magazine for the first time.

According to his own testimony, Ritwik wrote about a hundred short stories, and at least two novels—from 1943 onwards. Out of the short stories, some fifty were published in leading magazines like *Desh, Shanibarer Chithi, Parichay, Agrani* and *Notun Sahitya*. Unlike his attempts at poetry, Ritwik was self-confident in his experiments with this medium. He was to say later—in a moment of a rather modest self-appraisal: "The stories I wrote were not too bad!" In fact, they were of a high caliber, as evident from the immediate recognition they received in literary circles. Introducing one of his earlier stories to the readers, while publishing it in the well-known Bengali literary journal *Galpa-Bharati*, its editor, Nripendra Krishna Chattopadhya, described Ritwik as a powerful young writer.[6]

But his honeymoon with fiction did not last long. As restless as ever, Ritwik soon left this realm and moved over to another medium—the theatre. Explaining the shift, he was to write later: "... though literature is a terrific medium, it works slowly into the minds of the people. Somehow, I felt, there is an inadequacy in the medium. To start with, it is remote at the same time, limited to a very small readership, serious literature being what it is. Then came a revolution in our Bengal of that time. Came a new wave of dramatic literature led by Shri Bijan Bhattacharya of *Nabanna*

---

6. Re: Ritwik Ghatak: *My Coming into Films in Cinema and I*. Ritwik Memorial Trust. Calcutta. 1987. P 19; Chitrabikshan, op. Cit. P. 64; and *Ritwik Ghataker Galpa*. Ritwik Memorial Trust. Calcutta. 1987. 0.9.

fame. It revolutionized our way of thinking. I found that this was a much more potent medium than fiction and also most immediate. So I started writing plays, acted in them, directed them and did all other incidental things around a show. I became very much associated with Indian People's Theatre Association, in a nutshell, IPTA."[7]

It was finally films where Ritwik found his forte. But it took a heavy toll on his health and mind. He made films like one inspired, a man possessed with work and action. He created masterpieces. But few among them were to be recognized during his lifetime. As a result, all along his life, he had to fight to raise finances to make his films. After having made them, he had to face an unresponsive audience—'one great wall' as he described them in one of his most movingly written articles, where he also tried to reach out to them by appealing to their discerning powers.[8] Anxiety, frustration and bitterness drove him to alcohol. "Somehow I feel alcohol is the final road to salvation. I get engrossed in it, I really do."[9] But the frequency of these self-destructive fits could never stand in the way of his creating

---

7. *Chitrabikshan*, op. cit. P 64. Bijan Bhattacharya (who was later to perform in Ritwik's films), set the play *Nabanna* in the background of the 1943 famine. It became a landmark in the history of Bengali theatre when it was first staged by the IPTA (Indian People's Theatre Association). Ritwik himself acted in a later version of it. During his days in the IPTA, he earned fame by acting in Rabindranath's *Visarjan* and Gogol's *Inspector General*, and wrote a number of plays, out of which his staging of *Jwala*, *Sanko* and *Dalil* are still recognized as powerful theatrical productions.

8. Sari Sari Panchil in Ritwik Kumar Ghatak: *Chalacchitra, Manush Ebong Aro Kichhu*. Calcutta. 1382 (Bengali era).

9. Interview in *Chitrapat*, No. 10. Quoted in Shampa Benerjee (ed). *Ritwik Ghatak*, Directorate of Film Festivals. N. Delhi. 1982. P. 97.

some of his best films—most carefully executed—which were by no means morbid or unwholesome, but full of gentleness and marked by his commitment to humanism.

It was this commitment which made Ritwik return to his 'first love' sometime in the 1960s, when he produced a number of austere little tales and vignettes—tautly compressed and epigrammatic in intent. A few of them are included in this volume. His son, Ritaban (who has been tenaciously collecting all this writings, scattered in different places, and has published some of his stories and has made them available for translation in the present volume) informs us that in October 1962, Ritwik prepared an outline of a novel based on his childhood. In 1965, he wrote a long story entitled *Pandit-Mashai*, the manuscript of which was eaten up by white-ants! Thankfully, shades of the story can be recovered from a film-script called *Janmabhumi* which he wrote on the basis of that story, and which was published in *Abhinay-Darpan* in 1968. We are also told that between 1963 and 1971, Ritwik started writing new stories.[10]

We would have loved to follow the course of Ritwik's return to the realm of the short story. We would have waited with bated interest for the new experiments that he might have introduced after an exile from the medium for almost seventeen years. But his attempts were cut off by his untimely death. Ritwik Ghatak died on 6 February 1976. There is no use regretting what we have lost. One hopes that the entire corpus of Ritwik's stories—both published and unpublished - can be recovered and restored to us.

---

10. *Ritwik Ghataker Galpa*, op. cit.

III

The stories in this volume display a surprisingly wide span of Ritwik's concerns. Both in their style and their themes, they show considerable variety.

Some of the stories are set in Bengali middle class environs (like *Shikha or On the Trail of the Milky Way*), while some deal with working class people and their struggles (like *Comrade* and *Eyes*). Some are passionately romantic with a palpitating poetic quality (like *Ecstasy* or *Love*). Some are grimly realistic descriptions of social injustice (like *The Deposition*), and the human tragedies born of the 1947 Partition (like *The Crystal Goblet* and *The Earthly Paradise Remains Unshaken*). Ritwik combines these various tendencies with great power and tenderness in his stories—sometimes in the same story.

Incidentally, four stories deal with the theme of murder—*The Deposition, Comrade, Love* and *Eyes*. But they are not on the typical lines of a mystery thriller. The first three are murders committed out of love for the victims—a motivation which Ritwik delves into with a ruthlessly analytical bent of mind. The last story is of a different nature with political overtones, where the factory official puts to death a protesting woman worker, whose dying and cursing eyes continue to haunt him.

When we move beyond the stories of the 1947–50 period and read the epigrammatic tales written towards the end in 1968–69, we enter a different world. Although they suggest a continuity of the same moral and political ideas that we find in Ritwik's earlier stories, they seem to have been sublimated to a different level in these tales. Here Ritwik tries to compress those concerns within a few words. Can this ability to express the deepest thoughts in the most laconic terms in art be possible, only after the artist reaches a certain maturity towards the end, having passed through the agonizing odyssey of self-expression, which also involves self-discovery? We can recall the reduction of the human form almost to geometrical starkness in Michelangelo's last three Pietas, or the *Upanisadic* succinctness of Rabindranath's last poems. In fact, in an article written in 1969 (when Ritwik was writing these tales), Ritwik referred to his growing love for the verses of Upanisad, particularly *Isa-Upanisad* and *Katha-Upanisad*. Describing his search for a similar style of expression in his films, he wrote: "A language that would speak briefly, without being frothy, without screeching, which would be self-expressive, without the weight of allusions ... A language which is terribly powerful and can capture every mood in a patriarchal manner. A language that is apparently dry, looks like a subterranean river, but is succulent like the famous mango of Malda ... there is such a language born out of the white heat of inspiration."[11] We should also remember in this connection that in the 1960s, Ritwik had turned to making short films and documentaries. Both *Fear* and *Rendezvous* were made in 1965. These epigrammatic tales of Ritwik's, therefore, need to be located in this overall perspective of his general thought process at that time which was looking for an appropriate style of expression.

As mentioned before, the earlier stories which constitute the bulk of this volume, were written over a period of only three or four years, from 1947 to 1950, when Ritwik was just emerging

11. *Chhabi Kara* (Making Films). *Amrita*, Sports and Entertainment Special Issue, 1969.Reprinted in *Chitrabikshan*, op.cit.

as a creative artist. They provide us with the rare opportunity of meeting a young Ritwik—far away from the troubled and brooding soul that could create a searing epic like *Subarnarekha*, far away also from a personality riddled with anxieties that would drive him to utter despair and depression. But one can nevertheless detect in these stories, the basic moral and political concerns that led him later to make the films that would make him immortal. We find the same inclination for intellectual argument, the ever-present critique of social evils, the dreamlike blend of the romantic and the tragic, the nostalgic longing for a lost El Dorado, the undercurrent of satire—all that were to permeate his films.

The dream of an El Dorado—or the search for something beyond the present surroundings—had perhaps haunted Ritwik from childhood.[12] In his stories this dream quite often ends with the loss of innocence. The story 'Shikha' is a melancholy satire on such a loss. The little girl Shikha grows up as a wayward creature in a typical middle class family. She is the despair of her parents, who have given up on her, relegating her to the margins of their own polite society. But her own marginalization in her home also makes it possible for Shikha to empathize with the other marginalized sections outside her home. The plight of the

12. Mahasweta Devi, the well-known novelist and short-story writer, who was Ritwik's niece (daughter of his elder brother Manish Ghatak), and grew up with him, while narrating her reminiscences about Ritwik's childhood, recalls: "In our country home, the autumnal full moon would work wonders on our childhood fantasies ... The far off bamboo grove emerging as a dividing line between our village and the next, conjured up alluring images of El Dorado for us." (Quoted in Haimanti Banerjee: *Ritwik Kumar Ghatak: A Monograph*. National Film Archive of India. Pune. 1985).

starving old mother of the dead miner brings tears to her eyes. In her childish mood of philanthropy, she imagines that one day she will create a better world—and El Dorado perhaps—by taking away all the money from the rich and distribute it among the poor. These are dangerous thoughts! So, there has to be an end to Shikha's unruly temperament and restiveness—just as the rebels in every society have to be nipped in the bud. Her parents finally pack her off to an expensive boarding school where she is broken and bent into the desirable cast of a society dame, to be married off to a fabulously rich owner of mines. The story ends with a description of a party thrown by Shikha—in her role of the rich wife. She has invited her uncle (the narrator in the story), who remembers her as the wild, but sensitive, child of the past. He finds to his chagrin that Shikha has eminently lived up to fears that he had expressed years ago when she was sent to the boarding school: "... taking the girl away from the real world and putting her in the 'kingdom of snobs' tantamount to killing her. There she would learn how to dance, sing with a genteel voice, play Bridge with stakes, in time, toss off drinks with aplomb, but she will not remain the simple innocent girl she was ...".

Returning home from the party, the narrator fishes out the old photograph of the grubby little Shikha that he took many years ago. Gazing at it, he rediscovers "such a splendid pose, creating a web of illusion about a unique childhood." Remembering the past, he feels the "tremendous urge to ruffle her hair and take her into my lap." But then he realizes that his *Shikhamayi* (the word *Shikha* meaning 'flame') "has gone out." It is not merely the innocence of childhood that is gone, but along with it the flames of rebellion have also been smothered. The sensitivity to the surrounding social reality that was once integral to the child Shikha's mind, has been gradually destroyed by the training in the boarding school, and totally eliminated by the environs of her rich husband's society.

But the yearning to return to that world of innocence, for a revival of an El Dorado in some corner in today's world, continue to haunt the characters in Ritwik's stories. In *On the Trail of the Milky Way*, the young hero goes on a holiday to "a place you and I have always longed to go." It is an idyllic spot where the earth pours out its secrets, in hushed tones, into his ears, where it seems that life's journey and its goal have somehow merged. To complete the bliss, here arrives a woman with her children to spend the holiday. But Ritwik does not turn it into a love story. The hero is indeed tremendously attracted to her, but she actually reminds him of the mother of his bygone, forgotten, childhood days. An extraordinary relationship develops between the two—in which the love of a mother for her son and that of a brother for the sister merge into one. "Like two little waves their identities mingled and became one and ... they thus participated in what was the great, age old search of human beings ... in quest of the blue bird!"

The story could have ended on this lyrical note. But Ritwik brings it down to the harsh reality of quotidian existence. Our hero returns from his holiday, treasuring the memory of his recent encounter. When he hears that the woman has also come back to her home (in the same place where our hero lives), he rushes to meet her hoping to revive those moments of ecstasy. But he is in for a big disappointment. Welcoming him to her house, she just makes polite conversation with him.

"The person he had got to know during those marvellous days seemed to have got lost among a crowd of ordinary faces." His friend to whom he tells his story, laughs at the hero's illusions. How could he have expected to find in the present surroundings, the same woman whom he met in the 'land of the gods'—the realm where she fitted in, in those days? The loss is rooted in both the spatial and the temporal distance. Individuals can rediscover an idyllic past in a particular spot, and live in tune with that environment during the tenure of their stay there. But once dislocated from that place and time frame, and on return to their old surroundings, they sag into the same old life style that they are used to.

The search for an El Dorado merges with a yearning for a quiet retreat for self-introspection in *Solstice*—an intensely subjective story. It touches a chord in the memories of sensitive readers who can remember their own desperate yearning to escape from the mundane reality in their quest for something beyond the present, which perhaps gripped them when they were in their twenties—the age in which Ritwik wrote this story. A young student gets lost in thoughtful contemplation about the deeper meaning of life, the innermost essence beneath the surface. In his desire to explore this inner world, he decides to quit the city and go to his village home where he hopes to concentrate upon the thoughts that are bothering him, and ultimately find the elixir of his intellectual existence. As he sits in the train that takes him away from his friends and the city, he is momentarily plagued by doubts as to the wisdom of his decision. But he feels reassured by the sudden flash of lightning in the sky a symbol of the hope that illuminates his new path.

The narrative, more in the form of a diary than a story, is interspersed with arguments within his own self, as well as with his friends. Abstruse thoughts often give way to concise and acute observations of the surrounding reality, like the brief sketch of a bustling railway platform where the narrator-hero waits for the train. Sometimes a lyrical description of nature, like the one about his sister's garden which he waters every day, merges with memories of an idyllic past that he had learnt about from ancient myths. In his search for a deeper meaning of existence, the El Dorado of the future blends with the paradise of the past.

The conflict between an imagined El Dorado and the prosaic reality recurs in another story—*Ecstasy*, where Ritwik also takes a dig at the Bengali middle class' romantic obsession with aboriginal women. An ex-political activist, disillusioned with life, escapes to a tribal village in the hills, surrounded by forests. It is in the form of a long monologue—the lonely man's self-introspection and romantic imagination. The beauty of the natural surroundings overwhelms him, and reminds him of the poet Kalidas's lyrical painting of the landscape in *Meghduta*. Watching a tribal girl collecting water from a nearby waterfall, he fantacizes about her—imagining how she must be spending a life of innocent joy in her village, far away from the tensions of urban life. This vision of an idealized bucolic existence soon inspires our hero with the thought of marrying this girl and settling down there. As the moon rises, and the environment looks more romantic, he gets increasingly sentimental, and decides to go to the girl's village the next day, tie a garland of flowers around her coiffure, marry her and live with her in ecstasy! But soon after, a doubt crosses his mind: will he be able to live in happiness forever? The story ends on this note—a tragicomic anticlimax after the erstwhile ecstatic paean to the glories of tribal paradise! By drawing the story to such an abrupt close, Ritwik leaves his readers to make their own conclusions. Is it our wistful craving to stretch the borders of a moment of bliss to a state of permanence that destroys our happiness? Or, does the dream collapse at the slightest touch of the mundane concerns of everyday life?

The longing for merging into the innocence of tribal life in *Ecstasy* can be traced to the sense of loss of childhood values (as described in *Shikha*). As among tribals, animism forms a major part of the developing of childhood sensitivity—before the child's world gets fragmented by experiences. Is it this which draws urban adults to the spontaneous primitivism of the tribals? Or, is it the sheer exotic? Or is it the gross cupidity to exploit their innocence?

The story *Ecstasy* in fact, reveals an interesting facet of Ritwik's searching mind which was to reappear in his films later—his lively interest in tribal culture. One of his earliest films (after the feature film *Nagarik*), was a documentary called *Oraon,* made in 1955, on the life of the Oraon tribals of eastern India. In an article entitled *About Oraons (Chotonagpur),* written at around the same time (1954–55), Ritwik spoke about their dances: "These dances create that atmosphere which suddenly makes you aware that you are witnessing a scene which is as old as the history of man in India. The tunes, the sound, the spectacle make you realize what vigour and joy of life is. They are precious because they invoke in you the primary emotions .... Work and relaxation, worship and pleasure, these are so intermixed and so well balanced that the emotional disbalance, the greatest malady of civilized society, has very little chance to appear."[13]

These lines recall the mood of the narrator-hero of *Ecstasy*. But Ritwik was clear-headed enough at the same time to recognize the fragility of any hope of self-identification with this world of the tribal communities. In the same article, soon after the lines quoted above, he added: "But to give this picture of the Oraons, or for that matter any other tribal society, is to help develop another myth, the Noble Savage. Unfortunately this balance and harmony is most evanescent thing; like a delicate flower it withers at the slightest rude touch. And touched they are bound to get." Ritwik had an inkling of this way back in 1947, when he ended his story *Ecstasy* on a cynical note.

But a more poignant feeling of loss that overwhelmed Ritwik, and left an indelible mark on his films, as well as on some of his short stories, was caused by the Partition of the country in 1947—an event which he could never forgive, and accept with the sense of equanimity that many among us have adopted. He felt himself wrenched away from his roots—both emotional and intellectual. At least three stories in this volume deal with the events of that period, two of them directly concerned with the aftermath of the 1946–47 Hindu-Muslim riots before and during the Partition. *The Road* is a warm-hearted and deeply moving epitaph for a spirit of communal amity that has now become almost dead. In the riot-scarred heart of Calcutta, two young people run into their Muslim friend, Israel. Forced to flee his home in a slum to escape Hindu attackers during the riots,

---

13. Reproduced in Ritwik Ghatak: *Cinema* and I. Op. cit. p.99.

Israel has come back to find that his house in the meantime has been occupied by a family of Hindu refugees who have fled their home in East Bengal to escape the Muslim raiders there. A sad and angry Israel at first curses the family. But when he discovers that it consists of only a very old woman and her grandson, the rest of her relatives having been killed in the riots, his mood changes. He takes care of the woman as a loving son would look after his mother. As the basic human urge for affection triumphs over hatred, Ritwik ends the story on a dramatic note—the rain pouring down and the sounds of its drops on the asphalt road becoming the pulsating throb of millions on the march.

The other story, *The Crystal Goblet,* is set in Delhi. It is the same period. Following the Partition, thousands of Hindu families have fled West Punjab and converged in Delhi, living in refugee camps. The hero of the story narrates his encounters with two such refugees—one, a young mother who has become mad after having lost her child to the cholera epidemic that is ravaging the camps, and the other, an old man who is looking for a person called the 'government' who, he hopes, can get him back the belongings which he has left behind—a cot, two buffaloes, one plough and clothes among other things. The protagonists in this story are small and insignificant people, the step children of life, who are either totally unhinged by their traumatic experiences, or are trying to make sense of the chaos in a strange city according to their own way of reasoning.

There is an undercurrent of anger and bitter satire. Ritwik takes a swipe at the national leaders who have ensconced themselves in comfortable seats of power far away from these poor people who have been rendered homeless by the policies of these same leaders. There is also an element of self-flagellation. The hero, who feels disturbed by his encounters with the refugees, finally ends up at a party in the house of his relative, where while finishing a drink from a crystal glass, in the illumination of which everything looks radiant, he comes up with the excuse: "What else can I do?"

The third story in this group is *The Earthly Paradise Remains Unshaken,* which is about the resistance put up by the common Kashmiri people against the Pakistan-aided tribal mercenaries who invaded the 'Earthly Paradise' in 1947 soon after the Partition. Although written more than fifty years ago, the story reads as if it is all about what is happening in the Valley today. The ordinary Muslim there now, like the hero of the story, Maqbul Sherwani, is again facing bullets from another generation of Pak-trained mercenaries. His plight is even worse today since he is being victimized also by the security forces of the Indian government—the same government whom his ancestors like Maqbul Sherwani helped to fight off the invaders in 1947. But to come back to the story, it is a rather poorly written piece, and often sounds like the modern patriotic pulp fiction and films that have been spawned in the wake of the recent conflict over Kashmir. It is important nevertheless because it expresses Ritwik's political position on a major contemporary issue. We shall come to it in a moment.

The viewpoint chosen by Ritwik in these three stories coincided with the development of a certain socio-political situation in the country, and was rooted in a particular political approach that Ritwik was imbibing at that time from Marxism and the CPI. During the communal riots in Calcutta in 1946, CPI members played a leading role in resisting the rioting mobs in certain areas, rescuing both Hindu and Muslim families from affected spots, and bringing out peace rallies there appealing for Hindu-Muslim amity. This political spirit is reflected in *The Road*. At the same time, Ritwik uses the incident described there to make a larger statement—the universality of human love that cuts across religious and other barriers. The universality of human suffering is brought to the fore in *The Crystal Goblet*. Here is a young Bengali observer watching and empathizing with the plight of Punjabi refugees, uprooted from their homes after the Partition. I am not aware of any other Bengali writer dealing so sensitively with the sufferings of another community—who like the people from East Bengal were also victims of the Partition. I am also not aware of any non-Bengali novelist or short-story writer (particularly from the partition-affected north India) who has cared till now to delve into the plight of the Bengali refugees of that period.

The other story set in the background of the politics of the Partition, and situated in north India, is the one on Kashmir. What made Ritwik step out from his Bengali environs, and write these two stories—*The Crystal Goblet* and *The Earthly Paradise Remains Unshaken*? Both the stories have political overtones. We should not ignore their political sources. The CPI, with which Ritwik was associated, in those days brought up its followers on the belief in the solidarity of the common people all over India—irrespective of their religious, regional or linguistic differences. In keeping with this spirit, CPI cadres and sympathizers from the north to the south in India rallied together to raise money to help the victims of the Bengal famine in 1943. The solidarity of the toiling masses was further reiterated in the cultural activities of the

Marxist-oriented IPTA (Indian People's Theatre Association) of which Ritwik was an active member. This exposed Ritwik not only to the variety of the rich cultural tradition spread all over India, but also to the political developments taking place in different parts of the country. In Kashmir at that time, the Communists were supporting Sheikh Abdullah's National Conference and its resistance to the Pakistan-sponsored invasion. Ritwik's story on Kashmir quite naturally, therefore, reflected his sympathies—perhaps in a rather stridently melodramatic style that often jars on our sensitivities.

Ritwik's political views come out more sharply in three other stories—*Eyes, Comrade,* and *A Fairy Tale*—where he takes sides with the working class and their struggles. The first story is a deeply penetrating study into the paranoiac fears of a murderer. A supervisor in a textile mill, at the behest of his boss, kills a woman worker who is a trade union leader. He is haunted by her cursing eyes. The eyes multiply, when thousands of workers bearing the same gaze, close in on him. *Comrade* also deals with a murder. But here it is a worker who murders his friend and leader when he finds out that he is betraying the cause of the striking workers by selling out to the factory owner. He weeps while strangling him—determined to preserve his memory of him as a beloved leader, and wipe out his role as a blackleg.

Both these stories spring directly from Ritwik's own experiences of working class life during his stint as an employee in a textile mill in Kanpur. The third story *A Fairy Tale* is set in middle class surroundings, where an honest editor defies the owner of a newspaper, publishes reports and writes editorials in defence of workers' struggles, and is sacked as a result. He gives the owner a sound thrashing, and as he quits the office the workers of the press feel that "another soldier has joined their resistance army." The style is rather exaggerated, and sounds mock-heroic at times. But then, it is appropriate for the events that are described. As the title indicates, it is wishful thinking about a happy impossibility. It is the stuff that dreams are made of, for helpless intellectuals.

Even in stories that do not directly deal with politics Ritwik introduces social problems from a progressive political standpoint, like the impact of development on the common people, or feudal oppression of women. *The Tree* was written more than fifty years ago. Yet, it shows extraordinary prescience on the part of Ritwik. The events narrated look like an anticipatory reproduction of what is happening today—environmental and social disruption due to developmental projects that are out of tune with the psychology of the people. An old Banyan tree in a village, which had served as a landmark for visitors and shelter for travellers passing through the village, was felled to make way for a new developmental project of the government. The banks of the ancient village river were dug up and trimmed to turn it into a new-fashioned canal. The villagers suddenly recognized the importance of the Banyan tree—which they had taken for granted all these years—and realized how badly they would miss it. They protested. But their protests were mere murmurs. The tree was brought down, and after a few years of refuge in the memories of the old villagers, it silently disappeared from the mental world of the people.

In *The Deposition,* Ritwik achieves a dramatic intensity by making the narrator-hero kill the woman he used to love once, in order to put an end to her sufferings at the hand of her husband who had infected her and her unborn child with venereal disease. Brought up with the traditional ascetic norm of stealing her mind against all humiliation and oppression in her marital life, and accepting her fate, Jaya rejects the hero's proposal to leave with him, and also refuses to commit suicide to escape her fate. Unable to accept her subservience, the hero provides her with the only escape route available to her—an end to her tortures and future diseased life—by murdering her. After surrendering to the police, he requests them to give him another chance to kill Jaya's husband, while he remembers the stink of the burning food in her kitchen when he was strangling her. The stink haunts him.

This terrifying state of psychosis reappears in another form in *Touchstone*, where the protagonist is a connoisseur of music, but madly obsessed with the search for ingredients with which he hopes to make a medicine that will bring back life to the dead. Finding no chance of collecting enough money to buy the ingredients, he sinks into a mood of utter despondency. But the next day, he whips himself up to a frenzy of aggressiveness, attacks—only to remember with regret that he had thrown away the list of the names of the ingredients during his mood of despondency!

Unlike these two stories which touch upon the morbid, *Raja* is set in a lighter mood. It is in a class of its own. The poet-turned-pickpocket visits his old friends after a long time, and spends a delightful evening with them, exchanging reminiscences and impressing them with a respectable-looking fictitious account of his own life and home. Ritwik brings a sting in the tail of the story. Instead of ending it on the expected note of the pickpocket's loyalty to his old friends, he makes his hero remain loyal to his profession. Before leaving, with his dexterous and artistic fine fingers, he picks up a wallet from the pocket of the shirt of an unsuspecting friend of his, who is fast asleep!

When critically judging this main body of Ritwik's stories (written in the 1947–50 period), one feels that strokes of genius are often marred by trivial patches even by loud melodrama in some of the stories. In the political stories in particular, one may even detect a sort of innocent naiveté, when he ends them on the optimistic note of working class resistance—a concept, which we find today, is fraught with social problems and individual motivations that defy the simplistic belief in proletarian solidarity. But if sometimes the mood in these stories seems sentimental and the imagery trite, the rare power and conviction that they carry, and the breadth and variety of Ritwik's experiences, easily make up for whatever deficiencies one may detect in them. Besides, let us remain grateful to Ritwik for reminding us through these stories of the still necessary hopes and beliefs about an egalitarian society which remain hanging as frayed ends and tatters from a past dream of a socialist world.

But it is in his other stories—mainly of a subjective nature—where Ritwik reaches a level of far-reaching significance. A deep psychological insight into human impulses, accompanied by an exceptional gift of humorous focus on human moods, helped him to come up with some of his best pieces in this genre. A story like *On the Trail of the Milky Way* for instance, acquires a disturbing significance, which is profounder than an ordinary satire. In *Ecstasy* again, the romantic and the prosaic blend in a dreamlike atmosphere. An apparent triviality often expresses a deeper understanding of human motives, as in *Raja*. At the other end of the pole stands a story like *The Deposition,* which brings together two incompatible, but deeply associated themes—romantic love and domestic oppression of the beloved woman—to a deadly conclusion. Such stories convey an ambience of both self-introspection and an intense relatedness with the surrounding reality. The most representative of this literary trend of his is *Solstice.*

The stories written in the 1960s which are included in this collection, are bound together by a style of density and compression, which sets them apart from the earlier ones belonging to the 1947–50 period. *The Divine Resonance* glows with a concise brilliance, where the reclusive musician is awakened by the goddess of music to the shining beauty of a musical note, just by the touch of her fingers on the strings of the *veena.* Listening to it, the musician feels that this is the ultimate, the end of the world—just as Keats felt when listening to the nightingale: "Now more than ever it seems rich to die."

In *Love,* flaming passing contracts into a moment of violence, when the lover kills his beloved. Interestingly enough, *Love* is different from *The Deposition,* although both deal with a similar theme—the lover killing the beloved. While in *The Deposition,* Ritwik goes into an elaborate argument to justify the murder, in *Love* he just leaves the readers with an intensely stark description of the happening. Is Ritwik trying to attach here a deeper meaning to the relationship of the physical extinction of the body?

The didactic and the poetic become one in *Attack!* Ritwik uses the mythological story of Subhadra's abduction in an innovative way reversing the roles. Instead of Subhadra, Arjun sits at the back warding off the pursuing enemies. The story inspired the well-known artist Somnath Hore to do a sketch, showing a peasant couple in a reversal of roles while engaged in cultivation. It is the man (Arjun) who bears the plough, while the woman (Subhadra) steers the ploughshare (the chariot) to make furrows in the field, and a child (Abhimanyu) runs around them holding a stick. Explaining the motif in his picture, Somnath Hore said that Arjun was valorously carrying the plough under the stewardship of Subhadra to fertilize the field, and added: "Subhadra, Arjun and Abhimanyu with his staff—who on earth can defeat this powerful trio?"[14]

There is surely a political message in *Attack!*—which inspired Somnath Hore. The message comes out clearly at the end of the story, where Ritwik moves into the modern times. The story was written in 1969, during the beginnings of the Naxalite movement. The youth of Bengal, the Abhimanyus, about whom Ritwik talks at the end of his story, were already on the warpath, preparing to launch an attack on the moth-eaten old system and its institutions.

Being a non-conformist himself as well as a Marxist intellectual, Ritwik had an innate ability to empathize with these rebels of the Naxalite movement. He ends his story with the hope that they will launch the final attack that will make a dent into the *Chakravyuha*, the prison of our socio-political system. He did not lose that hope till the end. Five years later, after the writing of *Attack*, he was to return to these Abhimanyus in his film *Jukti, Takko Ar Gappo*, made in 1974. Meeting the Naxalite guerillas

14. The sketch, along with Somnath Hore's comments, is reproduced in *Ritwik Ghataker Galpo*. Ritwik Memorial Trust, Calcutta. 1987. pp. 126 and 129.

in their jungle-hideout, Ritwik, the intellectual Nilkantha, tells them: "In my Bengal, you are the only ones who mean all for me! There's nothing left," and then reiterates his old hope: "I'm sure you will snatch the future, whatever happens!"

Anatole France was believed to have said: "Let us give to men, for their witnesses and judges, Irony and Compassion." Ritwik Ghatak's stories reveal a deep emotional affinity with human virtues, and compassion for human frailties. There is also an undercurrent of irony that runs through most of these stories. Gifted with a sense of both irony and compassion, Ritwik bears his stories to their witnesses who are the readers, and to their judges who are the critics.

One hopes that the present collection of Ritwik's stories will win for him a wider audience among the non-Bengali readership. A translation is not merely carrying over a meaning from one language to another, but also conveying the spirit from one form to another. Rani Ray has shown enormous courage in her attempt to be faithful to the spirit of Ritwik's stories while bringing his complex style into an English version where his characters appear to move and speak with the same feeling and tone, as in the original.

Sumanta Banerjee

The Tree

Gachh

A banyan tree lay tumbling down on the banks of a little river, flowing by at some distance from the village—a tree about which one has little to say—an ancient tree with a termite infested trunk and rotten boughs. It must have stood ruddy and strong in some remote past; it doesn't now. The tree had no use for anybody. People on their way recognized the tree as they knew that Haru potter's furnace stood on the curve behind it , from where the road wended its way to the original village.

The tree became an object of pride only at one time during the year—during the *Charak* festival, when its roots were brightened up by oil and colour and people arrived from afar; a fair would be held on the village grounds. All of a sudden, the tree would become a sight to behold! Then for the entire year everyone would turn their backs on it. The cows would graze on the parched earth of the neighbouring fields. At times a distant traveller would rest under its cool shade, leave after eating *chire-muree*, tied up in a bundle and taking a draught from the stream.

Who knew what secret dreams beguiled the tree, gazing at the fluctuating currents of the river on a moonlit night when it fell prone in its own compound, next to the stretches of field and created a delightful play of light and shadow! The six seasons of the year waved past its head without a pause, boats sailed by in the river, little faces peered through the gaps of the boat covering and gazed at it in extreme curiosity.

The children made the bottom of the tree a place for their rendezvous. They would play about energetically on its branches, dive into the river from its boughs, bunk school and sit by its side.

The village folk were used to visiting the tree from their childhood. They had made a comfortable seat for themselves amidst the tree's tangled roots where they sat and listened to the soft gurgling sound of the water.

The fishermen of the locality knew they could catch fish in the gaps in between the roots that spread on to the bank—big fish and small. That was why their children trawled for fish with their towels when they arrived at the place for their baths. A lot of fish were caught in nets as well.

The old folk were familiar with the tree. They would sit leaning their backs against its stump and watch the boys at play, the fishermen would trawl for fish and nod their heads. Perhaps they contemplated the evening of their lives.

But even those old men had no idea how much space the old banyan tree had taken up in the life of their minds! They thought of it merely as Lord Shiva's old banyan tree. It had always been there and would no doubt exist forever. They thought that as they went past Uncle Haru's turning there would always be Shiva's old banyan tree!

And so it would remain standing where it did for the succeeding generations of men, and would give shelter to many would-be travellers in the future.

But all of a sudden without any prior warning the government's new plan made its presence felt, and according to the current irrigation scheme the river bed had to be widened. As a consequence the tree fell to the ground, making a huge racket, putting up a sturdy resistance—Shiva's old banyan tree! And a modern canal was constructed by digging evenly into both banks of the ancient river.

The entire village was stirred into action. People came to realise what the tree meant in their lives. Every village soul got agitated—they voiced their protest.

But their resistance never went beyond verbal murmurs. The tree fell down, and then slowly but surely the image of the tree faded from people's memory.

There were new faces, new houses, everything that was new. Only the old village folk found the place looking rather bare—empty when they went past by the river bank. That was why they would describe the tree to the new people, gesturing with their hands. They talked about the changing times. But how long could that go on?

The old banyan tree which had given shelter to so many in the past has now silently faded from people's mental horizon.

1947

Solstice

Ayananto

One particular day

The monsoon descended today; the white sails of little boats, unfurled against the backdrop of dark blue clouds across the Padma river presented a rare sight!

The landscape in front of me became a blur; a red road made a curve in the opposite side of the field; a tall krishnachura tree stood, apologetically—totally drenched. One or two labourers passed by carrying loads of soggy rice grain—the scene was hazy, hardly noticeable and the atmosphere peculiarly still.

Inside the lecture hall, the professor expounded the spiritual philosophy of Rabindranath Tagore. I heard his words but couldn't make sense of what he said. It was strange—I could see drops of rain gather and slide down the slightly inclined electric wire that ran like restless children from the Arts building to the Chemistry building, visible from my window. At places, blobs of water fell below.

The winged angels on the terrace of the Library building, still further away, were welcoming the sheet of rain. Among them was an angel with a broken arm—I felt such pity for her. She stooped; there was an air of helplessness in her pose. Splashes of rain fell on the windowpanes, drops of water rolled down the glass, smudging the scene outside. The sound of the continuous monsoon shower drugged my mind!

It was strange that in the somnolent state of mind I was in today, grief surged within me—a sense of a loss: something that had been but no longer was. As if time's tide was pulling me, along with the entire universe, to a place where the river mingled with the ocean; as if I was floating on a strong wave, desperately trying to hold onto the embankment, but helpless against the strong haul of the river current, managing to leave behind only the imprint of my five fingers on the sandbank.

Inside the room, the professor's voice was a relentless, quiet and serious drone; outside, the youthful clouds called. The sound of rain falling on the leaves of palm trees came from afar. A wet pigeon, perched on the cornice of the terrace, endlessly flapped its wings—my mind was crowded with curious thoughts. I couldn't bear to hear the incessant moaning of the monsoon skies any longer.

I came out of the college building with a strange sensation in my head—nothing pleased me; I felt as if I was in a stupor, as if I had no destination in view; thoughts like these kept churning inside my head. I recalled a philosophical principle: let things be where they are, moving them elsewhere is of no use. Today I sensed *that* was the truth. If only one let things be, one could succeed in avoiding future problems, save oneself from much futile exertion.

It had stopped raining. The streets were already muddy with water. Every now and then a gust of wind produced a sprinkle of rain from the palm tree leaves; the mournful sky was as sullen as before. The sky was overcast with formless clouds, giving it a grimy look. I went about aimlessly in the streets; I had no desire to return home. I wandered from place to place and came and sat next to the river. The sky cleared gradually; the flaming rays of the sun smeared the two-hundred-year-old indigo factory with a red colour. Dampness etched gray and white patches on its walls, and I remembered a day of my childhood when I had come down with a temperature. It was the monsoon season, like this one; the atmosphere had been full of moisture. The crest of the palm tree in the Library grounds had bobbed up and down. Lying in bed, I had woven so many wonderful dreams around the patchy walls next to my cot! I came to my senses, all of a sudden—the evening had grown dense. The shoals of Katalmari across the Padma had become indistinct. Lights had come on in the streets and houses in town. I walked home, heaving an expendable sigh. My head was throbbing; I had a foul taste in my tongue. I came and stood in front of the mirror and carefully scrutinized my reflection: a nineteen or twenty-year-old boy with restless eyes, of delicate build, almost thin you could say, looking tired and distressed. An ordinary boy with a longish face with a dirty twill shirt on; there was nothing to single him out as an extraordinary being.

I drew myself away from the mirror. I am often in this frame of mind when all kinds of peculiar notions jostle inside my head. I have the urge to go away somewhere, where only Nature reigns: the banks of the great Manas Sarobar lake, perhaps, where flocks of swans come to rest in early spring, flying over so many oceans and mountain streams, abandoning their happy retreat at the source of the Indus river; or where icy currents stream down, in slow rhythm, the sharp slopes of the snow-peaked Kailash mountain. I ate and went to bed. Didi had probably left a bunch of hasnuhana flowers behind. The room was redolent with a charming smell: a pure, sacred and exquisite aroma.

The rain ceased. I opened the window and a gush of mild moonlight fell obliquely on my bed. I put out the dim lamp. Outside, the night reigned supreme—the eternally enchanting night that cajoled the senses. The moon came up and revealed itself in the gap among the two rain-laden clouds. Crickets chirped endlessly at a distance. The *poetry of the earth is never dead!* A painting of the monsoon night by Debiprasad[1] that I had seen many years ago, in the magazine *Bharatabarsha* or *Prabasi,* came alive, suddenly, in my mind's eye.

I placed my hand against the window; the bright moonlight outside brought to relief the shadowy image of my hand. For no reason at all, I wondered about the simultaneous configurations of my hand as it appeared to me now. I was amazed at the thought of the multi-faceted aspect of my hand. I felt confused and mystified as I cogitated more about it. What appeared as simple on the surface was really baffling deep down! I felt an earthquake had shifted and shaken the ground under my feet. Thoughts such as these fill the mind with uncertainty and darkness closes in—and yet I believe one can overcome doubt by contemplation over a period of time and reach beyond the pale of ambiguity. But I am not at all sure where one would finally arrive—it is a question for which I have no answer. But I suppose one could shed light on the mystery and all such inconclusiveness if one

1. Debiprasad Roy Ghowdhury the famous Bengali painter and sculptor

were truly free. Our body—our physical existence—the mark of man's animality, places obstacles in the path. Man's weak frame cowers at the prospect of a regime of austerity.

I looked at the image of my hand carefully again; what I saw was merely a shape—an obstacle in light's way I realised. An ignorant child would take it that way. But if I were a physicist, I would be obliged to speculate differently; for instance, how a bunch of electrical nucleons revolves a million times around every single minute particle containing negative atoms in numbers that could boggle the mind. The contrary pulls of attraction and repulsion of the minute particles send forth waves of light which become the hand's colour. The atoms change places in each and every tiny molecule, without altering their place or consuming time. The molecule is of material or temporal nature—all of it was beyond my comprehension. To tell the truth I understand little, enough to want me to go mad.

The conclusion would be different if one regarded the phenomenon of the hand from the point of view of chemistry. The molecules would then be made up of several atoms, that revolve around a nucleus—these again form molecules of several elements. If I thrust my right hand into the fire, the molecules would get separated as atoms.

A biologist would regard the innumerable cells my right hand consists of and would discover that every cell has its own particular function, which it carries on without coming in the way of another cell. It works without making errors of any kind, by coming into existence, flourishing and multiplying. It works by combining its efforts with others like it, according to some pre-conceived design. If the hand got burnt the cells around the wound would give birth to new cells, gradually forming a tissue to cover it.

In this way the many conceptions of the hand, existing in so many worlds like electricity, chemical molecules or living cells, take their being in the hand that we regard as impeding the flow of the pale moonlight—the hand that is also an instrument to do good or evil. It exists both in the material world and in the life of the mind, simultaneously—as at this moment. The question naturally arises—what is the connection between the many forms existing in multiple phenomena; what makes a quiver in the heart merge with chemistry? I am faced with the mysterious depths of a dark and frothy ocean. If there is a harmony in the order of things, I have failed to see it. For me there is a world above another big world; layers piled over layers, although each stratum is separate and distinct. What is true for one stratum is non-existent for the other—and yet each stratum has its own reality and its right to exist. One cannot speak of a world using the terminology of another. Mind is neither chemistry nor physics—I know that much.

But where lies the key to all this mystery? Surely one can find some explanation for it if one thinks deeply. Perhaps everything is a part of the life of the mind, or has its existence on the level of the spiritual—all else is illusion—the superfluity of differences in the appearance of things. One has no right to declare this as the truth if one has not spent many years thinking about the problem, giving it one's undivided attention. The mind has to be free and expansive; it has to be charitable. These are, after all, my own notions. None of them has been put to proof to become acceptable.

Thus, I continued my mental search for the great meaning of life, while drops of rain bubbles pursued each other along the section of the wire visible from the classroom window. The patchy walls of the indigo factory, the angel with a broken arm on the terrace of the Library building, the shoals of Katalmari—insignificant details such as they are, jostled and revolved inside my head. I slowly fell asleep—I don't know at which hour. I woke up once, in the middle of night and found a splash of rain come into the room through the open window. I shut the window and lay down. I mused about the clouds that would form in the sky across the Padma river, the strange shapes of the buildings, the sound of the conch shell, the religious rituals, the din and bustle of crowds, and beyond all that, a line of mountains, leaning against the sky, obscure, wrapped in mist. A mild scent of hasnuhana hung in the air; the heavy patter of rain outside, the sound of the night bird flapping its wings on some tree, frogs croaking somewhere nearby, the intermittent wail of the next door baby—I turned to my side to sleep.

Disquiet

I was sitting quietly by myself when Ranjan and Kapil suddenly came in; Ranjan was a strange boy; he had a glowing, fair complexion and rather big eyes. He always looked serene; his eyes sparkled with intelligence. Gazing at him I would feel I had come face to face with someone who had espoused the life of an ascetic. He spoke little, if at all, stressing each word he uttered. One couldn't help noticing him in a crowd. People not familiar with him addressed him with respect. As for Kapil—the dark skinned, long haired chap was always in a light-hearted mood.

Once he started to talk he couldn't stop. He had an opinion on just about everything in the world, which he spared no effort in declaring. Although temperamentally poles apart, those two were soul mates. Life for them was one long celebration; there was always something to commemorate. They were constantly engaged in doing something, fearing they would lose their all if they were not thus employed.

"How is it that the two of you are here at this unholy hour?" I asked.

"Swami Sahajananda will be giving a lecture this evening at seven, in the college common room. You must come—a bit early, we both are the organizers, we need your help," Ranjan said.

"Very well, I'll be there," I said.

All of a sudden Kapil exclaimed, "Binu, you see to all that with Ranjan .... I have to be elsewhere ..." He had hardly finished his sentence when he left.

There was a total silence in the room. Ranjan sat with folded hands and looked out of the window. A little sparrow swooped down in the front and pecked something off the grass. A woodpecker continued to knock noisily against the trunk of a berry tree. The sing song voice of a boy reading for exams in a house nearby could be heard. Din and bustle were singularly absent in the little town.

"What's the matter with you?" Ranjan asked.

"Why do you say that?"

"You behave strangely; you listen to all we say and yet appear to be so indifferent. You talk in such an odd manner."

"I am suffering from acute mental anxiety."

"You can talk about it if it is not a deep secret."

I couldn't decide whether I ought to tell him anything at all. Who knew how he would react to my innermost feelings! I was extremely hesitant—felt as if I were a self-conscious young girl asked to face the footlights.

Reluctantly I began, "I have had this kind of feeling before; I had a recurrence of the same mood yesterday—a peculiar sensation, as if this earth, the stars, the planets and the sky were all being swept away on a surge—Have you ever visited Shillong in the winter? The inhabitants of that place claim that water gets coated with ice during the winter. Men on holiday skate on the wafer-thin ice which covers dark warm water underneath. We too seem to be hurtled along standing on the upper crust of this earth, not giving a single thought to the big world that is hidden beneath the bright mantle. But I believe that with some effort we might be able break the ice covering and then the life below will be revealed to us and we would see all that there is!"

Soon I resumed a normal manner and confidently said, "We only see the surface of things—we don't think, don't speculate—to imagine anything beyond what we see is prohibited. Yet little inconsequential incidents in our lives remind us of our myopia—I have had the experience time and again. I feel dizzy to think all that. Nevertheless, I think that if one tried to simply contemplate, leaving all else aside, day and night, year after year, one could perhaps succeed in penetrating the veil."

The room echoed with my voice; its sound was strange even to my own ears when I stopped. Ranjan looked at me in a queer way. It was drizzling outside, sounds of conversation in the streets floated in. I continued to talk.

"I have been thinking of only one thing these several days - you may think I am incoherent if I were to tell you what it is. Nature has the power to intoxicate us. The person who has once savoured the nectar of the earth is never free. Nature has drawn him unto herself, engulfed him completely. The beauty of the changing seasons, the brightness of spring, the noisy quiet of harsh summer afternoons, the incessant sound of rain during the monsoon season, the fields touched with gold in the autumn, fragmented clouds shrouding the deep blue sky, the dew glistening on blades of grass in the early winter morning sun, the ascetic indifference with which winter dismisses the riches of the earth I feel as if I am going mad—the same question haunts me over and over again—what is the truth behind Nature's numerous images?"

I stopped talking as abruptly as I had begun. Ranjan sat in the same pose, his hands on his lap, his head slightly inclined, his eyes smothered in drowsy silence. Who knew what his thoughts were? But it was remarkable how my cogitations had taken roots in his mind. The combined exertion of my many vocal instruments had sent waves of sound across boundaries of infinite silence and had created a ripple somewhere; the little waves of sound had with the help of other instruments entered his thoughts and had created a perturbation; because of it, his sleepy imaginings had come to life. I had sown the seeds of my ideas in his brain. Man succeeds in putting his own notions into the heads of others. That's why man dies—so that his thoughts remain immortal. Only for this reason man writes stories, composes poems, strums songs. He engraves the train of his mute thoughts on the mound of a hard stone with an even harder instrument. Because of such preoccupations of man we have come to know how the world appeared to him a thousand years ago. Taken aback I heard Ranjan say, "Do you know how long Gautam sat and meditated under the Bodhi tree?"

"I can't recall—perhaps twelve years."

"Twelve years?" Ranjan slowly repeated, stressing each syllable.

Some time passed; Ranjan muttered to himself,

"O Earth, you look back and read without gratification the same writing everyday..."

I looked up at him, speechless. His face and eyes were strangely bright. He looked abnormal. He got up noisely, "Let all that be—it's late—I'll be leaving now. Come at the right time tomorrow." He went out. I kept sitting as if I was in a stupor; then I too got up and left.

Didi had created a little garden in the patch of land in our house. I would go and water the plants every day before I went for my bath. I went to the garden today too, put down the water can and came and stood beside the well. A bhat flower shrub was growing nearby, it was in blossom. The air was full of a strong and sweet smell.

I remembered Rabindranath Tagore saying somewhere, "This world of ours is like the rich land of Lanka; the whole mind of man is captive to it like Sita in chains; demons are forever enticing man. But the cluster of flowers like the emissary of god Ram, taking cognizance of the situation, reminds Sita that she is in prison—freedom lies outside. That blessed freedom had to be won through pains. These wild flowers carry the message of the world at large; they provide a link—a bridge to life outside. We will comprehend its message only if we remain alert and we realize that this golden city of the demons is not all that there is—there lies the greater world of men outside its precincts, where love will succeed and our lives will be fulfilled.

Little, ordinary things of life—clusters of flowers, for example, are like poem fragments, which carry within them moving blobs of water. The sound of rain falling without pause on palm leaves in the nights of *Shraban,* the unending song of crickets—all illuminate our inner being. The feeling roused in us when we witness such phenomena is the same as the musical scale of the classical raga *Gaur Malhar*. It's an incredible feeling, taking the mind into the region of the timeless where at one time, there was a little garden bounded by a row of pine flowers, where the homing birds flitted restlessly to build their nests on the roofs of the village shrines at the onset of the monsoon season, where bears came down from the hills to eat ripe berries, dark as clouds, growing at the edge of the village, where the elders gathered to discuss the changing world, where the country women looked innocent and where the scent of aroma-filled hair floated out of palace windows, the house pigeons gathered on rooftops to sleep when the night was dark—There Shankar is lost in *Tandab Nritya,* the cosmic dance, holding aloft a bloodied hide in his two uplifted arms—in a land where exists Vidisa along with the fragrant streams—Darshana and Sipra.[2]

I settled down on the steps of the well.

---

2. Myth and legend, dream vision and literary reminiscence are blended in this description of nature evoking the topography of Kalidasa's *Meghdootam*. The *tandab* dance of Siva represents the idea of simultaneity and inseparability of creation and destruction.

In company and elsewhere

It was evening—I was standing beneath the tamarind tree, facing the college room. Swami Sahajananda hadn't made his appearance as yet. Kapil had gone to bring him. Quite a few people had gathered for a meeting such as this one.

The sky was a deep blue, as if a day in autumn had unexpectedly shown itself. Pieces of white clouds floated in the sky. It had rained heavily in the afternoon. Water on the leaves and the grass glistened in the sun. There was a happy feeling everywhere. A group of boys came forward and got hold of me. I went with them exchanging trivialities. Talk, jokes, bits of witticism, shouts and confusion pervaded the atmosphere—typical of men when they get together! The clouds had reddened in the light of the falling sun on the skyline at the opposite end of the horizon. Small birds flitted about restlessly on top of the tamarind tree. Nature seemed to be silently baring its many beauties, one by one, not caring if she remained unnoticed.

I tend to become absentminded when I am in the sun, I cannot fathom the meaning of nature's glories, nor understand the kind of longing nature evokes in me. Perhaps, I feel the emotional pull of the earth and sense that once I was one with the earth. There was some unspoken, subconscious life of which I was a part, that seeps through the grass and the leaves. The secret recesses of nature teem with life. I had always had a strange affinity with the natural world, a relationship hard to articulate. I knew that the people, who I moved with, at the present time, would think all this was gibberish. I can't bear the thought of rejection of the message of my inner soul.

Kapil arrived with Swamiji amidst much brouhaha. I saw Swamiji from a distance. I had heard he was a Harvard graduate who had lived in the USA for many years. He was a small man with a wide forehead that exuded intelligence. He wasn't handsome, according to any standard, but had something to make him likeable at first glance. He was always smiling.

The meeting commenced and Swamiji held forth wisdom, ethics of work, and faith, as these were propounded in the text of the Gita. Big words! Philosophical truths! They resonated faintly in my ears. I felt suffocated by heat, left the room and came out onto the veranda, unable to bear it.

A lot of time passed; the evening came upon us surely. A team of ducks, lifting shell fish from the pond waddled down the road, swinging; a herd of cows was returning home with a young cowherd driving them along with his staff. The assembly dispersed; there were shouts of people, noise of chairs and tables, Swami Sahajananda came out. Ranjan and Kapil went forward to see him off. Swamiji left in a car accompanied by another boy. The audience bade goodbye and left—the common room emptied out. Ranjan and Kapil returned.

Concluding our business, we went out together. It was eight in the evening—there were few people on the street. We walked in silence for a while when Kapil suddenly said, "I have heard everything from Ranjan. I had always thought of you as a normal person; no one would guess from your talk that you are such an ass. What do you mean by raising such fundamental questions—are you seeking *Nirvana*?"

"I am not going after *Nirvana* or anything like that, brother; these thoughts keep cropping up in my mind. I want some answer!" We resumed our silent walk. Kapil asked, "How do you intend to carry on your search for an answer?"

"I believe I can get to the bottom of it all if I contemplate day after day, year after year. I am thinking of retiring to my village home, and of staying there for some days. There I will think deeply—for a year or two, as much time as I may need. There are so many hurdles, difficulties, hindering my life here; I will be less troubled living in the village."

"But it is cowardly to run away like this—no one has the right to dismiss what ninety per cent of the people accept as reality."

"Why can't one? One has the right to become six feet tall, possess a fifty-four-inches-wide chest, doesn't one? Everyone can be one or the other. Then why can't one be born with the gift of thinking differently from others—have a mind which does not stop at perceiving the appearance of things?"

"Then will what millions of men unqualifyingly accept as the truth become a lie?"

"Why is that? There are many different ways to discover truth, to gain freedom. Every individual pursues the path he chooses—what he thinks as the true way is valid for him. This is not a matter for argument. Rabindranath has written:

My way to freedom is not one of self-denial
I will taste liberty happily among the
Many attachments I have formed.[3]

There are those who believe like him—my way is different, that's all."

Ranjan was walking without a word; he broke his silence now.

---

3. RabindraNath Tagore, *Naibadya*, 1900

"You live in your private, make-believe world—it will crumble with one push from the outside."

"I believe that will not happen. I will try my utmost to see that nothing destroys my faith. Perhaps, you think of me as a good-for-nothing. I indulge in day dreams while the whole world is hard at striving—I'm perfectly aware of it." He laughed at me, making me stop. Then I too laughed.

"You see the problem is that everyone now thinks that work is the most important thing in life, that one should be always busy with work—there is nothing else that has value. Those people have ninety-nine out of hundred ways open in front of them to choose from. I will take the one that they have discarded if the other ways don't suit me. I would have liked to have become somebody too—although I don't see much hope. To tell the truth I haven't put in much effort."

Ranjan spoke out quietly now, "My main objection to what you say is that you have only yourself to fall back on in your search—all ways out of yourself will be closed to you forever and you won't even know. You can't know who you are without interacting with others."

"That is no doubt true," I admitted. "One can't know aspects of oneself without coming into contact with others. But I have travelled in many places the last ten years, mingled with many different types of people; I am aware of the different sides to my personality—I don't think there is much I need to know about myself—there is nothing about me I can learn from others. On the other hand, there is the vast unknown world within me waiting to be tapped; it is a universe unto itself. To know that I have to submit myself to constant introspection. I am curious about myself—I want to know more about who I am. There are other reasons ... for which I must concentrate on myself. Unless one is fully self-aware one cannot fathom the mystery of this universe of ours. You may think I am talking big or babbling endlessly, but honestly these thoughts have created havoc in my mind. What else can I say ... you mustn't think I am insincere?"

We had neared Kapil's home; he bade us goodbye and left. Ranjan and I stayed behind.

Self-controlled and thoughtful Ranjan! He had hardly uttered a word while Kapil and I argued; he had just listened to our talk, paying attention to each word we spoke. I wondered what his question to me would be. But he didn't ask me anything nor said a word while he meandered along with me, his head hung low. With his arms crossed against his chest he seemed to be deep in thought. He placed a hand on my shoulder as we approached the bend where his house stood, then he looked straight into my eyes and mumbled a faint goodbye and left.

The decision

It had rained again last night. The lightning struck frequently, clouds roared; I heard sounds of falling rain from palm tree leaves in the field facing me. The night echoed with so many strange sounds. Flashes of lightning and the rumbling of clouds lent a wondrous aspect to the night.

It rained last night ... the incessant flow of water flooded and drowned the entire scene. Darkness descended on the field, dense and black. I had sat ruminating till late. The atmosphere surrounding me had opened the floodgates of my thoughts. Nature's sublime music outside—I in deep meditation, resting on my chair, with my hand poised against my cheek—I couldn't remember when sleep overtook me. I woke with the feeble light of daybreak, and discovered with sleepy eyes, the flickering flame of the oil lamp. I extinguished the flame and came outside. It was no longer raining. The day had not earnestly begun, only the darkness appeared to slowly fade away. I had the urge to play music after a very long time. I went inside and picked up my sarod.

Soon the room was suffused with melodious notes produced by the magical comingling of the dissonant strains of the raga *Todi*. I played for a long time. The morning mood created by notes of the *Todi* raga matched the state of mind I was in. It conveyed a message of emptiness to my heart. I went on playing the sarod. Soon the day broke and people came out on the street; the mid-morning rush replaced dawn's meditative mood. Another day had passed me by. A precious day in my brief existence had gone and I recalled a few lines of a French poem.

La vie est breve
un peu despoir
un peu de reve
e puis Bonjour

(Life is short, hope small, a momentary dream, and then goodbye)

I had read the poem in a Bengali book that day—a small hope—I knew I had only a little hope to reach my ultimate goal. I had neither the requisite wisdom, nor the experience. Perhaps my thinking had no validity at all. It was my utter ignorance that gave me a distorted view of life. I felt hopeless although I knew I had to carry on my search till the end. Nothing should shake my resolve—despair and fear were in store for me; I was prepared to face them. If I overcame fear and despair, unlimited happiness awaited me.

I had thought about these things till late last night, finally deciding I would tell my father and leave for my village home. I had nothing to tie me down here.

And then? What was there for me? Failure or success? I would go away for six months—stay longer if I needed to. I would only read and think about this world of appearance, its mystery, nature's various secrets. I had to have the answer—to my big question. I would take my sarod along with me for I would gaze at the many manifestations of the different seasons in rural Bengal with the sarod in my lap. I would strum the steel string of the instrument to welcome the seasons.

The earth would be hurtling forward, revolving in time; innumerable events, big and small would be taking place every minute in the churning of endless time in the infinite sky. How does the nebula or the amorphous mass of gas, self-engaged, produce the solar system; how does the constellation of Urs Major (the seven holy saints) leave a vivid trail of enquiry in the sky? I wondered also about the million light waves travelling from the distant stars, reaching and illuminating my courtyard, lighting up my eyes. I wondered about the time span of a journey that concluded at my doorstep.

The door latch rattled. I woke up from my reverie with a start. Ranjan and Kapil entered my room as soon as I unfastened the door.

"I have decided to leave for the village today—don't feel like staying anymore," I said.

"You are out of your mind, really I don't know what to do with crazy boys like you—Look at Ranjan—he has been sulking since last evening—won't talk," Kapil retorted.

Ranjan laughed, "Who isn't slightly off balance? You think yourself as sane but at times you act in a way that makes people think you are stupid or mad as a hatter.

"Let that be." Kapil changed the topic. "But I don't approve of what you're doing—I repeat what I had said yesterday—It's cowardly to run away from life."

"I have nothing to add—I know I can't make you think my way."

"I am an average human being, content to live like others. love life as it is; I don't think I have lost out on anything by not discovering worlds beyond the world."

"Perhaps, you are right. But how am I to know whether you are right or not? That's why I have to find out for myself—maybe I will retrace my steps, follow you. But let me say this to you—I too love this universe of ours, as deeply. It's like enjoying a song being sung well, applauding and saying it is wonderful, relishing eating sweets. Knowing the ephemerality such things doesn't prevent our enjoying them. We love to read a good book without believing a word it says. I too love this earth, our life—the music and rhythm—so what if all this temporary. It's wonderful this savouring of life ... how can I possibly complain—I who am temporary?"

Kapil went on nodding; he didn't like my arguments but was hard pressed to give a suitable reply.

I was fed up with all the talk. I felt it would have been better if I had left quietly without announcing my departure plans. I was being unnecessarily held back.

Kapil didn't utter a word. A lot of time passed; silence reigned supreme except for the sound of our breathing. I gazed at Kapil's face: he looked so serious, absorbed in thought. As for the eternal charmer, the handsome Ranjan ... he was looking outside, sad and pensive, a faint smile played around his lips.

All of a sudden Kapil spoke out harshly, as if he was trying to rid his mind of pressing thoughts.

"So ... you are leaving us, finally. We'll have to arrange farewell party for you, don't we? You needn't worry about me. We are not yogis, reflecting on matters of the spirit."

Don't weep for me ...
I have my duty, I have the world and its people
Goodbye, my friend![4]

His voice sounded pathetic in spite of himself. I kept on looking at him. He could hardly speak. The room echoed with pitiful silence. I felt as if these two boys were a big part of myself—I would face a void if they were not around. I had thought I was free of all emotional ties; I discovered it impeded every step I took.

The house for which I had never spared a thought, the little garden where I watered the plants, the old calendar aslant on the wall—all small and insignificant details of my surroundings suddenly became voluble. Perhaps my test would begin right here, in the breaking free of these little ties. It was necessary in order to discover that which was the sum of life or the elixir. If I come to know the One that is above and subsumes all that lies

4. Rabindranath Tagore, *Sesher Kabita*, 1929.

below, I would rise above time and space and conquer death, and that would be achieving the elixir.

Kapil and co. got up now. I accompanied them to the front gate. Walking down the street, they gave a backward glance.

"The train leaves at seven pm ... you both must come and see me off," I shouted. Ranjan nodded while Kapil stared vacantly. Locking the gate, I came back to my room.

I am sitting on a bench at the station with hustle and bustle surrounding me—crowds of passengers, some exchanging blows in front of the ticket counter. Kapil and co. are nowhere to be seen. I sit in silence among hectic activity, placing a little suitcase beside me. A porter passes by carrying luggage, a person calls out to his companion on the other side of the platform. A gentleman comes out of the crowd gathered next to the ticket counter; he counts his change holding on to his ticket, his nose in the air. The family sitting next to me must be his, a shy veiled wife, a small child, mounds of luggage. The child screams, the wife talks to the child in a hardly audible voice. The gentleman sitting on the trunk with its colours peeling off, fans himself with the end of his dhoti pleats. The place full of impossible noise, traffic and people's voices. I look on idly.

There is a football ground across the railway track. The bamboo posts stand firm although one has a broken cross-bar, a babla forest rests at its back with an oak tree standing solemn letting down thousands of hanging roots. Marks of age are etched on its trunk, millions of fallen leaves are scattered at its feet. The twilight pales into a grayish colour. Why haven't the friends come? It is almost time for the train.

Two countryfolk standing next to me are having a row over money for the ticket. The commotion is more than I can bear, a crowd of noisy men press in. I get up quite disgusted and roam about the platform. Every spot is occupied by one or other band of travellers, gossiping. I walk to the end of the station and stand placing my hand on the board that carries its name. A mild wind is gently blowing all over the place. Somewhere in the forest an unfamiliar bird whistles; it sounds really sweet. I remember again Keat's saying, *The poetry of earth is never dead.* I am amazed to think how the big forest in silent meditation looms next to such a big town, bustling with activity. The oak tree must have stood like this when I arrived here first, when I was admitted to school, and even when I was born. Perhaps every one of its millions of cells were generating newer cells when my father was being born. It is in this way that vital beings are assembled and sustained.

Thoughts invade my mind; they tumble over each other, unconnected and discrete like a film collage that rushes through the screen. But I am enjoying the mild breeze, and suddenly I am awake. Someone places a hand on my shoulder. I look back and find Ranjan and Kapil. Ranjan is happy, his face a picture of contentment. Kapil buried in thought, his brows knitted.

None of us speak ... it isn't necessary, it is odd to talk precisely at such a moment. I smile lightly.

But I am not likely to forget the scene—Kapil gazing far deep into the edge of the forest and Ranjan looking at me fully in the face, as in a painting, a little smile playing around his mouth. How bright are his eyes, I think.

The noise of the train breaks into my musings. The train sides in. All the shootings and the commotion that seemed to have got lessened now becomes strong. I go into a compartment carrying a suitcase in hand; they accompany me.

The compartment is dark. They come and stand next to my window. Kapil is looking away; he gives me a brief glance and lowers his eyes. Ranjan suddenly grips my wrists, "Wait for me—I will be with you ..."

I don't give a reply, just nod my head. He mutters indistinctly, "I will come surely."

All of a sudden he turns away and goes towards some distance. But Kapil keeps staring at my face, he looks really strange, his lips quiver for few moments, he looks appealingly at me. Am I going to pieces? Emotion is welling upto my eyes. I have to control myself, O god!

Ranjan comes back and takes hold of Kapil and firmly draws him away. I hear them walk away—Ranjan's steady footsteps, Kapil's. A strange sound rises from the coarse sand of the platform as their feet treads upon it. They go out of the station; they drop into the street. The road curves against a broken wall. I can see the bend of the darkening road from the window in my compartment. Did Kapil look back at me as he went around the bend?

I am overcome by a melancholy mood. I feel I am leaving behind an old and intimate life and will now embark upon a new and strange world. What will be the outcome of this estrangement?

Sometimes I think nothing will come of it—I am being very stupid. The compartment is now plunged into darkness. Clouds hang low in the sky, a flash of lightning rents the sky, a cold wind flows in. In the distance the blackened outline of the horizon looks smudged. It is going to rain—an answer to the prayers of the parched earth. Perhaps I have made a mistake: that's what I think, and yet gazing at the lightning-lit-up sky, I have a faint hope.

1947

On the Trail of the Milky Way

Akash Gangar Sroty Dhorey

Once upon a time a youth had gone on a holiday to a place you and I have always longed to go. At times you may have relished the experience of being there—in your imagination. This story has come to me straight from the boy's mouth—listen to what I have to tell.

To reach the place one has to get on the train, then go first by car, afterwards by foot. The place is full of mountains and wild woods. A comfortable bed awaits you there if you manage to get thus far, crossing the vast road. The bungalow consists of a room stuffed with furniture and a veranda, with a roof made out of red Ranigunj tiles. Its doors and windows are green, the walls are spotlessly white, like the foam on the crest of a wave. There's a little garden in front of the house, hedged by henna shrubs; a red-graveled road wends its way from there and reaches a little mart.

If you stood by the window you would notice the uneven ground rolling out at the back of the bungalow, beyond that the deep bed of an archetypal mountain stream, and an ash-coloured mountain range disappearing into the far-away deep blue horizon.

It was the end of summer when the youth arrived at the place; there was not a trace of cloud in the flaming copper - coloured sky. The dried-up river looked like the image of Parvati in supplication for a glimpse of the rain-god. The place was not too far from Ramgiri; had the youth pushed the time back by two thousand years he could have easily assumed the role of proud Yaksha, intoxicated by his own powers.[1]

The boy had reached the place after three days of arduous travel. It was night time and the moon had just come up behind the hillocks. There was no sign of any human habitation near by; the entire universe was enveloped in a dense darkness. Perched on a highland tree, a moon-besotted bird poured out waves of heavenly music. Perhaps a sambar had passed by, trampling the dried-up leaves, as a crackly sound emerged from the dark pile, while leopards grunted from afar. It seemed to the youth that the forest land that had thus far lain silent, like discarded, withered leaves, had slowly begun to find its voice; that wilderness itself, teeming with life, had turned restless. An enigmatic unvoiced message was relayed to his soul. His heart twinged in pain as he heard the motherly call of the primitive earth.

'There's a spirit in the woods!' It pervades the grass and the foliage, the night's mass of clotted darkness, the smoldering brilliance of harsh afternoons, the shades of trees, and each

---

1. Ramgiri, Rama's hill and a place of his exilehood. Parvati is one of the many mythical rivers mentioned in *Meghdootam*. Yaksa, a pre-vedic figure associated with forces of nature.

and every forest blossom. All throb with an inner life. With the journey over and done with, the youth had sat languid on a cane chair in the veranda and was gazing at this profound rendition of a world in repose. The earth poured out its secrets, in hushed tones, into his ears, in the midst of the unfamiliar environment; the youth felt as if he were gradually merging with throbbing nature.

As he looked up, he saw the Moon god, the 'King of Night', in his orbit, moving towards the northern hills, and its radiance creating the illusion of a rainbow on the faint vestiges of clouds scattered here and there. An oblique light fell on his courtyard. The construction workers, sitting in half-shadows of the henna shrubs, were gossiping softly about their country; light from the lantern placed in their midst fell on their high-cheek-boned, brown faces—their eyes glittered in the dark. To the youth all this seemed fantastic. Memories of that first night comes to the youth's mind even to this day when one talks about one's native land.

He had sat ruminating in his chair even though his eyes were heavy with sleep. His mind was assailed by a single idea: he had seen so many countries, mountains and forests, towns and villages, the sea and the rice fields—all, but it was the first time in his life that he had this strange feeling—that the world of anonymous beings was what mattered and not doing anything or any other thing—the rude aspect of his surroundings was declaring this truth to him. The fact that he was alive was the final wisdom, unexpectedly revealed to him in the darkness of the night. It seemed to him as if life's goal and the passage through life had merged and become one. It was not some kind of a philosophical wisdom that he gained, but something he felt in the blood—this I can swear by whatever oath one wishes to make in the law court. The youth was incredibly stupid; he didn't have the intelligence to make it all up.

The next morning the youth was standing by a railway station. He had gone off to sleep at some indefinite hour the night before, and was woken up by the welcoming touch of the hot sun. He remembered he had to travel on a truck to a place, some twenty miles away, to attend a festival being held there—Our hero was extremely enthusiastic about such doings! He had come to this railway station, in the foothills, after a jerky ride on the bus packed with people. Now he was waiting for the arrival of a group of train travellers he had to escort to the place.

He stood enjoying the cool air and the quiet, peaceful ambience of the place; there wasn't the faintest sound coming from anywhere, only the gravel-threaded road reverberated strangely when he walked. All of a sudden he stopped dead in his track and listened to the sound his feet made, pressing down on the earth. Snatches of conversation in chaste *Urdu* floated in. Perched on the sholai tree on the back of a tawny mountain, a bird chirped without pause; a mild unpolluted breeze blew in—the youth felt rather nice.

Then the train arrived and the arrival bustle momentarily overtook the entire station. The youth attended to the noise for some time, then quietly moved near the truck. Next to him a single *palash* tree blossomed in the bare, harsh landscape. The youth felt captivated by the beauty of its red clusters.

The leader of the group came and placed a hand on his shoulders—he turned round. That's how he saw her for the first time. It seemed to him as if she possessed the beauty and the splendour of the *Kojagori* full moon night—during the months of *Ashwin* and *Kartick,* when goddess Lakshmi was worshipped—that much I have been able to draw out from the youth. I don't know why he had used the simile to describe her. I suppose because his linguistic abilities were rather poor! But he thought that, that one phrase captured the essence of the woman's beauty.

This is not a love story—it wasn't love in the ordinary sense of the word. The woman was married and older than our hero by four years. She had brought along with her three children besides. It's true our hero was tremendously attracted to her. But after the initial shock had subsided, he came to realise that his feelings were rather odd. You may describe that feeling as 'love at first sight' only if you concede that it defies the usual definition of the emotion, because the moment the youth saw her he remembered the mother of his bygone, forgotten, childhood days.

There are some women in this world who have this inordinate desire to overflow with motherly love. The youth recalled his unremembered mother and was filled with an intense longing—This was how they first met—you follow? Then they all went and stayed in the big house where the festival was held, he along with a gaggle of the young and the old.

The youth had some fixed notions: one of them was that a person who couldn't mingle with small children was not to be trusted; another, that coyness in the matter of eating was not only foolish but offensive as well. Holding on to such beliefs our young hero romped about the place with an army of youngsters, within an hour of his getting off the train and gobbled up twice the quantity of food as others, at meal time. The woman was serving the food. I think she held the same view as the youth in this matter. The difference between them worked to the youth's advantage; she loved to feed others, he was overwhelmed with feelings.

The emotions the youth felt deepened during the few days he stayed at the place roaming all over the mountain in a car, visiting a waterfall and generally spending time merry making. The woman had caught his feelings and she gradually entangled him in a strange and an irresistible attraction. Standing in front of a waterfall, on top of a marshy cliff, in the heartland of the forest—where nature was yet unspoiled and where peacocks and leopards roamed—with the deep blue sky above their heads, in the late *Jaistha* month, the two souls accepted each other. The indifferent world around them had no place in their thoughts. Like two little waves their identities mingled and became one, forming a small part of an extended, all-embracing eternity. They thus participated in what was the great, age old search of human beings: *the lost souls strode, hand in hand, shoulder to shoulder, amidst the wilderness of this indifferent universe in quest of the blue bird!*

The woman had but one sister in the world who lived somewhere with her in-laws. Every year her heart stung with pain on the auspicious 'brother's day'. But that day she anointed the dusky youth by releasing the floodgates of her pent-up emotions. The faded image of a face with a deep sindoor dot, that flitted in the youth's mind, coalesced with the features of the beautiful woman. An extraordinary relationship sprung up between the two—one that partook of the love of a mother for her son, a brother for the sister.

Some days passed and the youth accompanied the woman to her house near by. There, he met a lot of people who became unusually fond of him because of his sense of fun, his songs and laughter and his abounding affection. There are so many stories about how he roamed all over the place at nights driving the hillman sphinx, carrying the Winchester-Murphy on his shoulders—incidents that have no place in our narrative. Only one deserves mention.

The woman had kept melted chocolate in the ice box in order to freeze it. It was eight in the evening. Our hero unable to control his temptation wandered into the dark room and was happily licking chocolate off his fingers when closing the door of the fridge, he inadvertently let the glass slip out of his hands and smash on the floor. The voice of the housemaid made him frantically look for ways of escape, and to his horror he discovered that he couldn't locate the door in the inky blackness. He quickly crawled beneath the dining table, garnering a Nainital potato on his head in the bargain. He had managed to get under the table in good time; the maid had come in, switched the light on and left the place after driving out a cat. By this time, an icy cold current was running down the youth's spine and his head had swelled up like some kadamba flower. As the maid's black feet disappeared beyond the threshold, our hero gathered himself and came to the balcony at the back of the room. He switched on the light and sat down on a chair assuming the pose of a poet. The pounding in his heart lessened after a while; he felt comforted by the idea that the evening's misadventure would be attributed to the cat.

There was a call for dinner, and the youth entered the dining room for the second time that evening. As soon as he went in he found all the members of the family assembled around the dining table. Only the woman was standing looking stunned, with an open ice box in her hand. Our hero sat down making the usual remarks about the weather. All of a sudden he became aware that the woman was staring at him, her eyes open wide in amazement. He began to feel terribly self-conscious, but before he could guess what the matter was she had come and stood next to him. His eyes followed the gaze of others and came to rest on the shirt he had on; the chocolaty—brown spots all over it told their own story—rather pointedly. That finished him. He hardly knew whether he was alive or buried alive. Things didn't go on like that forever. The woman took hold of his hair and made him knock down the entire quantity of the remaining chocolate with utmost care and tenderness, putting an end to all his fears of being buried alive. The entire household convulsed with laughter.

That night, suddenly past midnight, the youth was wide awake; he had been sleeping outdoors. The sky was radiant with the moon at its peak; the sounds of wagon shuntings in the station yard penetrated his ears from the dark shadows of the valley below. There was a strong breeze and his mosquito net kept puffing up. He got the feeling he had left the earth behind and was travelling upwards, among the clouds in the vast emptiness of the sky, that he had risen above the sullied and turgid earth and was floating beyond the shadowy realm of the rainbow, close by the region of immense peace and all-pervading eternity. Stars glittered around him— the celestial bodies playfully flung their beams. It was a region where the giver was given due recognition for bestowing gifts with feeling, where those who had lost all got back what they had been deprived of, where fulfillment in love and success in life awaited him with garlanded outstretched arms, where faded stars and music, that had been stilled, assembled, and there was simply no end to the festival of lights. The youth's heart was filled with an inexplicable joy, and he remembered once again that 'being was more important than doing!'

Some days passed without notice—I'm sure those days were also crammed with incidents, big and small. The youth had little to say about them. He would suddenly stop and sit in silence, with his hands folded on his lap, while relating one or other of the occurrences.

One day, about the same time, shutting the bedroom door, the youth came and lay on the floor which was as cold as his mother's chest. He was surrounded by a battalion of sleeping kids: some actually asleep, others plotting mischief while pretending to be dead to the world. Wearing a red-bordered saree, letting her hair down and reading a book, the woman was also sitting near him, with her legs outstretched. Outside, the dust storm made a hissing sound; at intervals the cleaning noise from the railyard below floated in. All of a sudden the clouds roared and the first spell of monsoon showers descended on the earth. The youth went out quickly—opening the door, letting the moist cool breeze flood the room. Looking up he perceived the enchanting kohl-tinted clouds inclining towards the North-East, the abode of Lord Shiva. Waves of joy suffused his entire being; he felt like wandering out of the place like a peacock, spreading its multi-coloured plumes. The woman had come out and stood next to him—her hair was billowing in the wind and his nostrils were hit by a beguiling smell.

Waterfalls in the mountains frolicked with the advent of the monsoon rains; the youthful exuberant mountain stream pranced down the slope till further below—it was time for our hero to descend from the land of the clouds. His holiday was over—he had to get back to the workaday world, find the ground under his feet, by slow degrees. *Oh wearied, he is wearied to death!*

The youth returned from his holiday with one idea stuck in his head. I would like to put that on record: He said, "all of you insist that the past is past, nothing recurs. To that I reply—that may be true, yet it is the past that is eternally embodied; the future is uncertain. The comingling of past, present and future is but another meaning of emptiness. But the past is in itself serene, motionless, and certain; one cannot change it. 'We know nothing of the morrow but time is ours.' The image of the past in my mind will stay forever. It has a quiet beauty of a definite and particular kind which can be clearly grasped. Humans possess their past; it's all they have to call their own."

It would have been really nice had the story ended here. But our hero was rather stupid—hadn't I said this before? That's why he rushed to see her when he heard she had come down to the plains. He was in for a big disappointment. The woman smiled, asked after his well being, directed pointed questions at him, fed him with this and that—but she was not the same. The person he had got to know during those marvellous days had got lost among a crowd of ordinary faces.

The ass! He didn't realise he had visited the land of the gods, where she properly belonged. How could he find *that* she here—or now—Was it that easy?

1947

The Deposition

Ejahar

Yes, it is I who is responsible for the deed. I, Bhabesh Chandra Bagchi. My father is Gopesh Ranjan Bagchi. We belong to Rampur, Boaliya. I committed the crime—knowingly and in a state of sound mental health. I am making this statement fully aware of the consequences of my confession; I am making this statement of my own volition and not because I am under any pressure. I am guilty—note that down, police inspector—and now, tell me, haven't I acted rightly? There's no way I can remedy the situation.

Jaya was frightened out of her wits; she lived in perpetual fear of death. That's why I had to do what I did—but tell me, how can I stop grieving for her?

I've known her since she was a child—she was a year or two younger than me. We grew up together. I loved her a lot! Her sufferings made me feel only more wretched. She suffered, as all Bengali girls do because of their husbands.

Jaya was married rather late, when she was past eighteen. She was good looking; finding a rich groom wasn't problem. The groom, however, was rather old, on the wrong side of forty and a widower besides. To the family, in a state of dire poverty, the groom appeared like heaven's benediction. It was only I who had objected to the marriage proposal. I had just got home after a stint at the medical college, and had come to know about it. But my cavils bore no fruit. I have always had a violent temper; I go berserk when I'm angry. So I stamped out of the house and went westward with a job.

I had received a letter from my mother some days ago saying that my father's illness had taken a serious turn. Father had always been sickly; the summer's heat might have aggravated his illness. I was given to understand the situation this time was rather grave. I knew father's illness had no remedy; there was nothing for me to do when I came home except sit quietly by his bedside. Suddenly I was seized with a longing to see Jaya. I hadn't set my eyes on her for such a long time! She lived in an insignificant little town where the mail train never stopped, but there was a passenger train—the journey there and back was a matter of twenty-four hours. It was already evening when I got off the train. The place had an unusual charm; I felt very elated.

But no matter how alluring the place, Chaudhuri Mashai wasn't a pleasant sight! That gentleman was sitting in the front room of his ancient, dilapidated house including a courtyard, facing a pile of official papers and records. He was ugly as a tortoise; a big, fat, stocky and dark complexioned man whose head could hardly be distinguished from his shoulders. He was six feet tall and had surprisingly thin legs, like bamboo poles. I thought he looked rather odd. He didn't appear to be a man of education either. Perspiration, black as coal tar hung on his forehead. His voice was gruff—I suppose that was to be expected. He carried on a money-lending business with the peasants at compound interest.

Trying to be as friendly as possible, in the circumstances, Chaudhuri Mashai got up and taking a corridor, latticed with light and shadow, led me into the interior of the house. I had already made up my mind about his ugliness. Observing his features, from the outer corner of my eye, I came to the same conclusion. He dragged his left foot; it was deformed.

He talked about all kinds of things—said he was leaving for a distant village that very day to attend to property matters. He hoped I would stay back for some time. The climate was really healthy at that time of the year. He had to request me to remain seated in the front room while he was out of the house. He had to go—as his work didn't brook any delay. That was Jaya's room; she wasn't in—she must be busy with work. She should be back any time now. Unfortunately, he had to leave. In the meanwhile if I could ...

I kept sitting by myself for some time. Peering into the inner courtyard of the house I saw some clothes hanging on a coconut string tied in one corner. Then I noticed empty liquor bottles lying in the room where I was, and I became absent-minded. Suddenly I heard voices, which sounded like the noise made by the rattling of bell-metal pots.

"The woman has become really audacious! I say ... how long does it take to wash up these few pots and pans? Did the Ghose bloke make his round of the river bank today?" Someone replied in a mumbling voice. Then the shouting resumed.

"Enough—don't make an unnecessary show of affection. What can one expect from the daughter of a petty, low-class father?

How can one hope she will have a noble outlook? I say ... if you are a penniless beggar why reach for the moon? Such a charade! Showing off her learning as if all the erudition would take her to Heaven. What she needs is a few thrashes of the broom."

I sat astonished as the participants of the dialogue appeared, unexpectedly, in front of my eyes. The old story, I said to myself—in plain speech, a spiteful accusation! Wearing a tattered saree, Jaya was perspiring profusely holding onto a collection of pots and pans. A middle-aged woman, her hands placed on her haunch, in a familiar brawling pose, was indulging in a delicious tongue-lashing. Jaya had been beautiful as a girl; now she looked dry as chalk. Her eyes were sunk, her hair unkempt, and her complexion had turned a jaundiced-yellow. The hemoglobin count had gone down.

Jaya ... so many of my happy childhood memories were wrapped around her! Her whole frame had exuded such a motherly feeling. Chaudhuri Mashai had, no doubt, married her for her looks. But she was a veritable goddess Lakshmi who could, with a touch, bring peace and prosperity to any household. But that was something Chaudhuri had not discovered.

Jaya! I felt like laughing my head off. Unknowingly, I came out into the veranda.

She was taken aback by my sudden appearance.

"You ..." She said, "Come, let's go in."

The middle-aged woman probably felt embarrassed. Covering her face with her saree, which left a large portion of her body in view, she made enquiries about me in a low whispering voice, then left the place. I came back into the room. Jaya joined me there after disposing off the utensils. I learnt from her that the woman was

Chaudhuri Mashai's aunt—the household consisted of only the three of them. Such a big house! Jaya had wandered alone among its crumbling walls with banyan and fig trees forcing their way out of the crevices. Jaya said she did all the housework while the aunt sat counting her prayer beads and abusing her in the most filthy language. Chaudhuri Mashai, preoccupied with making money and collecting interest, couldn't be bothered.

She was delighted to see me. Pushing the lock away from her perspiring forehead, she asked, "When did you arrive? How's Baba? He has written about Khuku's illness ... how's she now?" Jaya gave my face a look over. "How thin you've become! All the irregularity ... you are tyrannising over your body—how can you expect to remain healthy? You do whatever you like, there's no one to control you. That's why you've lost so much weight in such a short time. In this way you're bound to fall ill."

I couldn't tell her that there was someone else who looked worse than me, who had become thin and emaciated and was inching towards death. Jaya was anxious about news of her family; she kept on asking after her friends and her companions—as she blew into the flame inside the wooden stove—she was warming the water for tea. I sat on the mora and told her what I knew. Jaya went on chatting in her typical manner, inclining her head sideways. I gazed at her neck, it was so shapely, as if it were carved out of ivory!

Chaudhuri Mashai came in after a while; he discussed politics while he drank tea. He jogged my memory about the journey he had to make to a far-away village. He had to depart immediately. It was good I had decided to come. They won't be left by themselves. Jaya, of course, was used to being alone in the house when, travelling to distant places, he had to absent himself for a day or two. He lifted his canvas bag and bade goodbye.

I began to interrogate Jaya; I had to find out about so many things! I got to know that Chaudhuri Mashai drank quite heavily at times. Pishima always berated Jaya in the most vile manner. I had heard only a fraction of the abuses she hurled at the girl; she was capable of much more. She made uncharitable remarks about Jaya's father's pecuniary circumstances. Jaya had had to endure much these past several months. Suddenly, catching the look in my eyes, she stopped saying more. I must have looked severe and pitiless.

Jaya tried to change the topic and raised other subjects—her home, my job. The evening wore on. It became dark and Jaya left to prepare the dinner while I kept sitting where I was. Such a revolting situation! I had never, ever in my dreams imagined any one could revile and torture such a sweet and gentle girl like Jaya. I started to pace the floor.

I recalled what I had heard during her marriage—something quite abominable! Chaudhuri Mashai's first wife had committed suicide. I now knew the reason behind her taking that extreme step. I had heard that she had become mad before she took her own life.

But all that seemed insignificant compared to the contemptible state of affairs I was now witnessing. I re-entered the room where Jaya was; I had paced to and fro for some time. The aunt was nowhere to be seen; I didn't know where she had gone. I was barefoot—Jaya didn't realise I had come up right behind her. She was cooking with her back towards me. I wanted to ask the question I had forgotten to ask.

Chaudhuri Mashai walked, dragging his lame foot, I recalled. The walls of the kitchen were damp and infested with cobwebs; the unsteady oil lamp made Jaya's shadow vibrate on the walls. A portion of her body peeped in-between the gap in her clothing. I saw what I had to see: an ugly black mark.

"What's that, Jaya?"

I asked. She gave me a piercing look, startled by my voice. I had seen that look only for a split-second, a look that couldn't possibly belong to the girl I had known all my life. She hastily resumed her normal attitude and said, "It's nothing, really."

"Why do you say it's nothing? I can see clearly ..."

The truth tumbled out after much entreaty. Chaudhuri Mashai beat her with his shoes at nights when he was drunk.

Ughh! The veins inside my head began to throb violently—I felt darkness closing in all around me. Jaya got up to settle her rumpled saree. I saw everything, as if in broad day light—became aware of something I had least suspected. I hadn't been thinking in that way, perhaps because the lamp was throwing slanting shadows, or perhaps ... The knowledge that Jaya was pregnant came like a flash. I abandoned the idea of asking her any more questions. There wasn't any need to ... To me she was soiled, she had become debased.

I hadn't lost my senses. On the contrary, I was sure about the step I would take. Everything appeared eerie in the red glow of the kitchen fire and the wavering flame of the wick of the oil lamp. Jaya had gripped my hand in acute distress; the vegetables in the pan had shriveled up, giving off a peculiar smell—That smell haunts me even now, inspector—Ah! What was I saying?—Yes, I heard Jaya say, "I've found my solution. I've been taught by my father and know how to control my feelings and stay calm. Father interpreted the wisdom of the *Gita*, the *Vedas and the Upanishads* to me, on the eve of my marriage. I can bear all the insults in silence. I have done that till now. But I was badly shaken when I saw you here today, and my resolve had begun to falter. But it's momentary and has passed. It's not a serious problem anymore."

I bent my head and said in a quick, eager voice. "Hope is not dead as yet, Jaya. Perhaps it's not too late. Come with me now ... let's go back to my house."

"That's not possible," Jaya spoke in a quivering voice, "It's out of the question! It would have been a good thing if that were possible. I would have been saved. No, no, in spite of everything this is where I belong now."

"I feel like finishing off the bastard Chaudhuri!"

"Don't talk like that ... would you rather I was a widow?"

I got extremely anxious. My temper somewhat cooled, I kept thinking about the human beast Chaudhuri Mashai was and what more he was capable of.

Jaya had stepped back a few paces, she was looking at me steadily now, her large eyes opened wide.

"Suicide is a crime!" she volunteered.

I laughed, "Why is that?"

"One doesn't know when one might be of use to the other person."

"To whom?" I was about to burst.

"You too have learnt from my father, yet you don't seem to have imbibed his lessons."

That was no doubt true. I had spurned his wisdom.

"There's another way ..." I spoke out softly and drew near her. She didn't understand what I meant. Her neck looked tender but firm—cold as marble, despite all the pain and sufferings. I didn't have to press it too hard, my long fingers dug deeply into her throat.

She had an astonished look on her face. Her eyes were gaping and her hand held mine in a fierce grip—See, inspector, these are the marks of those nails ... they haven't gone away as yet—Could I have a glass of water, inspector?—Yes, Jaya was dead. I was without any feelings. I left the room carrying her limp, senseless body in my arms. The aunt couldn't be seen anywhere ... I didn't have a clue where she was.

I don't know whether I did the right thing by killing Jaya, but I felt it was the only way I could allow her to attain peace and freedom keeping her dignity intact. I was suddenly filled with an urge to remain alive and hurriedly left the place. I glanced back one last time at the house. In the half-shadows of the evening, the house with its long, extended veranda and crumbling walls was transformed into a ghostly place, spectral like an abandoned graveyard.

I walked to the railway track carrying Jaya's lifeless form. I knew sooner than later a train would pass that way—Have you ever sat beside an unfamiliar railway track with the body of your beloved in your lap? I have—so listen to what I have to say!—

The mingling of blue and black colours made the sky appear a slate-grey. The white clouds had moved far away in rows of long lines. There was no moon in the sky. The distant landscape came into view in the soft and hazy light of the blinking stars. Next to me, the bare, leafless and unsubstantial *babla* tree stood phantom-like in the dark. Clusters of sebai bushes—some fresh green, others robbed of all colours—thronged my feet. The water in the pit in front of me was as black as ink. The two steel lines of the track extended and blended into the dark. Night's moisture glinted like morning dew on the track; muffled noises floated in from a distance, and a cold wind spurred up.

I closed Jaya's eyes. To tell the truth, the look of fear in them had already gone and in its place was peace and quietness. Her tongue didn't roll. Only her incomparably lovely neck had become bloated. That didn't worry me—she looked so innocent and content. I patted her head lovingly for a while; her hair had become coarse and stringy. She had neglected to oil it for such a long time. I rubbed the sindoor off her hair-parting; it didn't become her. She looked nice, really nice! Jaya the virgin, the emblem of joy and well being! Forgotten incidents of the past days came alive in my mind's eye. Above me, the benevolent sky with its millions of stars shed its love over the entire cosmos. I sat with Jaya's head in my lap. A lot of time passed that way—nothing disturbed the peace that prevailed over the entire universe in view.

The moon came up, slowly brightening the eastern horizon—a running train illuminated the northern skyline. I lay Jaya on the track with utmost care and patted her forehead lovingly. As the rail lines began to vibrate with noise and movement, I touched her for one last time and came and stood behind the babla tree—Inspector dear, the train left ... I felt as if my heart had emptied out—There was such a void in me as if everything had gone blank! Jaya's body sliced into three pieces lay abandoned in the moonlight. I didn't look in that direction; chasing the railway track I stumbled into the station in a comatose state.

I don't remember how long I remained in the station. The railway quarters on the other side of the platform became visible in the oblique rays of the young moon. Gradually crowds of people assembled on the platform. I got up and retired into the corner of the shed. There was a foul smell. I wondered where it came from and glanced at the railway quarters. But the lights of the buildings were off. I couldn't bear the stink, felt as if I would suffocate. The train arrived after a while. I bought a ticket for Calcutta and boarded the train. I knew I wouldn't return home. I wanted to buy a stolen revolver from an acquaintance who lived at the end of Harrison Road. I had to have it no matter how high the price. I realised, that in terms of physical strength, I was no match for Chaudhuri Mashai—Is that your house? The one beside the police station? What a nice home you have, inspector!

You nabbed me at Ranaghat station ... but won't you let me go now? Give me some free time this once? I want to settle scores with Chaudhuri. He's a beast, ridden with unmentionable disease for philandering all his life! He has given his wife the same disease—his children were bound to be deformed. Jaya would have suffered hell had she continued to live! Chaudhuri was fully aware of all this. I want to release all the bullets into his body if you let me off for some time. I'll aim at his leg first, his stomach next and then his chest—Inspector, won't you let me be?

But what's the use of killing him—what good can come out of it—nothing! I have sinned, inspector, in taking Jaya's life. There are so many Jayas in this world, beasts like Chaudhuri! But have I done anything wrong? I have seen what suffering does to people—the agony father endured, year after year, when he lost his job. At least I have saved Jaya from facing utter ignominy. That look she gave me in the kitchen brought back memories of my father's stricken face.

I know you'll have me hanged—get on with your job, inspector! I won't suffer more than I would have had you throttled my neck with your two hands, like a pair of pincers.

I'm fed up. I have nothing more to add.

Inspector—run to your house and tell your folks to stop all the cooking! What a nasty smell of charred vegetables! Run fast.

1947

Shikha

I have her picture in my hand—a head full of hair, some of it falling on her face, her forehead and cheeks. One hand holds a plate; the other is pushed into her mouth. There's a suppressed smile on her plump face; her eyes are full of mischief.

Her name: Shikha. Looking at her you may think that the name is highly inappropriate. But a minute's acquaintance will make you realize its significance; the girl is hardly seven years old, a tiny tot, but she can be so boisterous! I remember the time the picture was taken. I had come to the terrace, camera in hand, to see if I could get a nice view of the mountains. I saw Shikha, sitting under the harsh sunlight on any empty terrace, behind the attic room, leaning against the wall single-mindedly licking something, and I was rather surprised to find her in that state in the hot afternoon. On precise observation, I discovered that the girl was swallowing huge quantities of a concoction of smashed mangoes, chillies and salt. I must have made a faint sound—I caught her eye.

I was simply captivated by the rare comingling of curiosity, embarrassment and apprehension on her face at that particular moment, and couldn't resist taking a picture of her. This is it: the photograph capturing to this day an afternoon redolent with beauty and flavour, the secret guzzling moment of the little girl's life. The I of those days has simply slipped into oblivion ... and the girl, where's she today? But looking at the snap-shot I feel I've gone back in time to those days!

My elder sister's daughter—I had seen her only once, a long time ago, when she was a child; I haven't set my eyes on her since. They lived so far away in an alien territory. I was a student at a Calcutta college. I had gone to visit my sister soon after I had taken my finals. I saw her, saw too the situation she was in at her home. If broken glass lay splintered on the floor, it had to be Shikha's doing; if food went missing from the larder, there was no doubt at all Shikha was behind it, if the children were late returning home, Shikha was held responsible for their delay. The girl was also strange—she sat mum, without demurring, all the more while she got roundly criticized. She refused to say what had actually taken place.

But I couldn't hold back when Didi got ready to beat her up in front of me one day. I asked, "Tell me Didibhai, what has the girl done?"

"I've had enough," Didi replied. "She pesters me all the time. I'd gone out only for a second, leaving the rice outside, because your jamaibabu called, and I came back to find the rice strewn all over the room, and her, absorbed in reading, sitting in the living room!"

"Oh dear!" I said, "But of what use is the rice to her? It must be the cat or ..."

Didi's voice rang out loudly like a bell, "You've no idea what she's like, Bhabesh—must she sit and read at this unholy hour, for no rhyme or reason? It is she who is ..." Didi's voice turned soft. "Do I beat her up for my own pleasure? After all she's my only daughter and yet she causes me so much distress. Hang around for a few days—you'll know what all she's capable of." Didi went out of the room dispensing with Shikha.

The girl had been standing, all this while, pulling a long face. She hadn't spoken a word or looked up. I drew her gently to me and made her sit on my lap. "Well Shikha," I said. "Everybody scolds you, don't they? Nobody is ready to listen to you." That slight show of emotion achieved what all the shouting couldn't: Shikha lifted her grimy face, with hair falling all over it, and looked up weepily at me. "It's true, Chotomama, can't you see they scold me for no reason at all. I haven't done anything."

I ran my fingers through her hair and brought it back to some shape, I said, "You don't understand a thing about all this, isn't that true, Ma?" Instantly Shikha lapsed into a sullen silence. "How could you ... you were reading at that time," I hastily added. Quite suddenly her small face brimmed all over with naughtiness. She spoke out, "I didn't chuck the rice purposely, Chotomama—it fell aside when all of a sudden my hand jerked, while I was carrying it in my frock. But tell me, Chotomama—if one doesn't do anything wrong, intentionally, it can't be sinful, can it?"

I understood fully the point she tried to make, but she was on to something else by that time; she was blabbering without end.

"Come, let me take you to see the pit. There are jet black coals there. It's pitch dark inside but the air is so cool and fresh!

The men are plastered with coal-dust. Do you know—Dada is so grown up but he gives a start, even now, whenever he comes across them. But me ... I'm not one bit afraid of them—I know them all. They live in mud huts over there ... I'm great friends with Kaushalaya, a girl who lives in that place."

By Dada she meant Master Tathagata—that young hero was of nine. Shikha continued to talk enthusiastically, rolling her head, going off on a tangent from one topic to another. Moving my fingers tenderly through her hair I kept looking at the way she panted while she talked, the enchanting way she paused to take breath, her delicate baby-like face turning red.

Her father came into the room - and said, "Bhabesh you here, already! What is this ... what's the brat doing in the room? Go, get lost." I could see her becoming tense, sitting on my lap. "Shikhamayi, go and change your clothes. They've become very dirty." I told her. Spiritless, she dragged herself out of the room.

Turning to jamaibabu I asked why Shikha was being treated like dirt. She didn't belong to a poor family so that the thought of her marriage could not already cause them anguish. Besides, she was their only girl child. Jamaibabu said, "What do you know ... the girl is the root of all mischief. She is the ring-leader of a puny gang in our house. She's really troublesome, beyond all control.

What could I say—she was their daughter!

At home, I noticed that only the grandfather was somewhat under the girl's sway. That gentleman, instead of 'retiring to the mountains', as they say, had nicely ensconced himself in one corner of the house, relinquishing his business matters to his son, and hanging on to his grammar book; his moustache was intact. The gentleman recited grammar throughout the day and thought there wasn't another humorous being like himself on this earth. Shikha would appear in front of him, suddenly, like a comet—whenever she chose. Then the pages of the grammar book would flutter in the air and his well-trimmed moustache droop. But he had no respite. The moustache would get pulled at, from time to time, and he would feel terribly flustered.

I had felt very bad seeing the girl treated thus. Her grandfather was with me in this. He wasn't an aristocrat, but a self-made man. That was why he could be sympathetic and open-minded about everything. I could see even he was helpless when it came to facing his son or the daughter-in-law. Shikha had unbounded spirit—wouldn't she behave badly if she was not allowed to go her own way? Her parents didn't understand that. The family were rich; they felt constrained about the girl getting too close to the earth. Shikha too was the limit—powdered in dust, and defying all norms and commands, she would carry on a secret friendship with Kaushalya, a labourer's daughter. She would push aside her Whiteway Laidlaw toys and cram her playroom with bits of stone chips, sprinkled with quartz and mica particles.

I'll never forget what happened one day—there lived an old woman in those parts who was called Jhabbu's Ma. She was known to me. Her son Jhabbu had died when the number three inclination of the mine had collapsed. Jamaibabu had tried to suppress the news. He lamented afterwards that it wasn't possible to live in peace with all kinds of envious people about him. The news had somehow reached the ears of the State's mining officer, who was a Bengali. Jamaibabu thought he was hard to please—the man wouldn't be bribed. Realizing that there was no hope from that quarter, Jamaibabu invited his wife home, addressed her endearingly as 'boudi', and successfully swept the affair of the mine-collapse under the carpet by making her happy with food and the gift of a necklace. There was of course a talk of compensation, but that had not got translated to action till that day.

One day Didi declared loudly, "She looks piteous, no doubt, but she is adept at stealing. You see, she got caught red-handed when she tried to get away after stealing a cloth. Your jamaibabu is such a noble soul—that's why she was only taken by the scruff of her neck, given a few blows and thrown out of the house. She had protested, saying she was cold and that she was merely taking a torn saree she had found abandoned in the courtyard, and would have told us about it. A lot of people make up stories for fear of getting beaten up," Didi concluded.

That's for sure! I had no two opinions about it.

One day, I took Shikha along with me. I was strolling towards the mountains, in order to reach a temple nestling among its peaks. The road was extremely narrow. A mound of granite stood high on one side; a heap of straw on the other. Jhabbu's Ma came upon us on a bend. She was leaning on a stick and couldn't see anything in front of her. She recognized me alright. She scolded me, "My boy, I've had no food for two whole days. I had gone up to the temple today—there was no food there either. Give me something to eat so that I don't go hungry." Her wrinkled face and doleful expression evoked a feeling of pity in me. I could see she was avoiding my eye, she was embarrassed. I had heard stories about her arrogance—an arrogance which was founded on her pride in her son. Son Jhabbu had been her life's glory. He had never drunk, had never blown his money thoughtlessly like the other labourers, he could sign his name in English. I took out a few paise. She brought out her feeble, trembling hand from beneath the tattered saree and held it out. I gave her an anna and immediately her face, covered by a multitude of lines, became suffused with a unique blend of smile and tears. She revealed her tobacco-stained teeth and said, "Live long my son, become an emperor." She wiped her tears and moved falteringly towards the slope.

I kept thinking that the woman had had no one save Jhabbu to look after her; and now that he was no more, it was surprising she could manage her days! In a flash, I recalled my obese jamaibabu and the anemic looking mining officer. I turned to Shikha. She was standing quietly—she hadn't stirred. I held her chin up and looked at her face—I found her eyes filled with tears, her cheeks wet. "What is it, my dear? Why do you cry?" I took her into my lap and rubbed her cheeks dry and continued, "What's there to cry about? I've given her money—she can buy something to eat now." All of a sudden Shikha brushed her tears away and began to titter like a grown-up woman. I put her down and resumed walking; she popped the question. "How many beggars are there like her?"

"Plenty, my dear."

"One hundred—two hundred, seven?" the numbers increased as I kept on shaking my head.

"Many more," I said finally.

"When I am older I will give away all of Baba's money to the poor—I'll feed them all," she muttered to herself.

"There are more beggars than your Baba's money can provide ..." I interjected.

"Then what is one to do?" She spoke out in despair, she looked worried.

"If we can get hold of all the rich men, take away their money and distribute it equally among the poor, perhaps then, the problem might be solved."

Assuming a solemn tone, she retorted. "Oh, I will snatch away money from the rich when I am big and give it to them." Swinging my hands, she sauntered gaily, happy to have dispensed with a knotty problem.

A total oblivion—following that incident. I can remember only the day I saw her for the last time. My examination results had been declared and I had done well. I had to get back to Calcutta directly to take a decision on my future. I was packing my suitcase when Shikha fell on my shoulders, and put her arms around my neck. I didn't utter a word, just ruffled her hair. I was moving my hand away when I felt her wet cheeks.

I put her down gently and cradled her. "My dear, you'll miss me when I'm gone, won't you?"

She wept copiously, hiding her face in my lap, I was silent. Some time passed. Didi entered the room, about to say something. I hinted at her to remain quiet and she left.

Shikha looked up. "My dear", I said, "You can write, can't you? Write me a letter—I'll reply."

Shikha shook her head violently. "No, oh no, I'll come with you." I felt a big hassle! I said, "Of course you will, but I will have to go first and arrange everything for you. Then I can write a letter to your Baba to bring you there, do you follow me, my dear?"

I was able to escape her clasp by such inducements. The same day I left the place.

I got a letter from Shikha a few days later: uneven alphabets by a tender hand. The page was torn from an exercise book.

Chotomama when you take me there, I not like stay here. Found a pretty stone by me an aeroplane tip for Kaushalya. Well is ma, Jhabbu's ma dead. Ma buy a Gokul Chandra record. Your Shikha

There was some scribbling next to the words. I studied them carefully; she had tried to sketch an aeroplane.

I received a letter from her father along with it. Among other things, he wrote he was sending his daughter to a famous boarding school. The name he mentioned was the place for the children of the very rich. My impression of the place was that you could find everything there except learning and humanity. I discovered Shikha's grandfather also held the same opinion. Jamaibabu was determined to send his daughter there, in spite of his father's objection. I replied almost at once. I said taking the girl away from the real world and putting her in the 'kingdom of snobs' tantamounted to killing her. There she would learn how to dance, sing in a genteel voice, play Bridge with stakes—in time, toss off drinks with aplomb but she would not remain the simple innocent girl she was. But who pays heed to those words! I learnt much later that she had been sent to the place.

Today—it is fifteen years since that time. So many things have happened to me during this period. I was away in the States for a considerable number of years pursuing higher studies in Botany. Back home I have a job as a professor in an undistinguished city. I immerse myself in the mute kingdom of plants in my garden when I'm not at work.

In the meanwhile my side whiskers have gone grey, my face has many lines, and I am not even aware. My parents died before

I went abroad. My brothers are carrying on their job of living, fanning out all over the country. My only sister, Didi, lives far away. The cacophony of voices of the spirited young boys and the silence of the variegated plants combine to fill up my life's cup.

I had seen my sister once after I returned from that country. My didi along with Jamaibabu had come to receive me at the Howrah station. Jamaibabu looked even heavier commensurate with his mounting bank account; his sense of decency had decreased proportionately. I was told that Shikha had been married off to a fabulously rich owner of mines. His name was Sailen Banerjee. She had come out of the boarding school highly accomplished. She was very happy—that's all.

I am in Calcutta today after a long time to look up some books in the Imperial Library. By the afternoon I had finished doing what I had to do. Back home in the evening I found a letter waiting for me—a short note from Shikha, written in a great hurry. She had written to say she was sorry not to find me at home. I must surely come to her house in Southern Avenue in the evening.

I go there. A palatial building with front lawns, a badminton court kept ready for the night's game, and swanky foreign-made cars parked in the portico. Two huge English dogs greet me with a loud growl as I come up on the varendah. A well-dressed servant comes out and looks disapprovingly at me when he finds I don't carry a visiting card. He takes down my name, comes back with a grumpy face and leads me inside.

So many creatures are seated in the room. The furniture loudly declares fabulous wealth and the lack of taste—simultaneously. Expensive drinks and snacks are served on a tray. I sit quietly in one corner. Shikha enters the room in what seems like a long time.

Yes, it's Shikha, no doubt at all! A deep red saree is tied around her body according to the new fashion—there's more of her outside the blouse than inside it. Her lips are smeared in a garish colour. She has shoulder length hair. She looks like a clipped, carefully preserved flower from her own garden.

She laughs holding a person's hand as she enters the room. Her laughter rings a bell—reminds me of the old days. Perhaps it's those dimpled cheeks that does the trick. She comes to me straightaway, and makes an effort to bend down. I don't let her. Her companion says something. She blurts out, "O shucks! No more please!" And turns towards me. "What a long time it's been! Sal is not at home, else I would have introduced you. These are my friends. I am 'at home' today ... Will you have a peg? It's real Golden Sherry, won't you? Hock? Claret? At least some Ginger ale?"

I shake my head, say I don't drink. She laughs revealing her pearl-like teeth, and rests her manicured fingers on her cheeks in a casual manner. "You're still so old fashioned after all those years in 'merica-and all that sort of rot!" She has a clipped accent, as if she's trying to impress.

But she has hardly any time for me. Her flock of friends are restive. "Doesn't matter ... sit for a while, don't leave, please. Feel yourself at home—please." She drawls out the last word In a sing-song way.

I leave the moment she turns her back. I know she won't feel my absence.

I come home and take my favourite photograph out of the drawer. A picture of the Shikhamayi who was mine—I gaze at the much-looked-at two and half by three and half piece of paper once more. It's an ordinary faded snapshot taken many, many years ago. What a lot of naughtiness in the eyes! A hint of smile on the cheeks—such a splendid pose, creating a web of an illusion about a unique childhood! Looking on I have the tremendous urge to ruffle her hair and take her into my lap.

But my flame—Shikhamayi—has gone out!

1947

Ecstasy

I have escaped to this place, where life is a sparkle and a thousand and one problems don't raise their heads every moment of my existence.

I was known as a flag-waving patriot and during the August freedom movement was even imprisoned once. I had laid down my life for my country. Now all that seems rather strange—so many years have passed since that time—I have suffered so much pain. Anger and hurt have slowly awakened in my soul—I can't bear to see all the tears, all the sufferings around me anymore. Inwardly, I have become increasingly intolerant. That's why, at the first opportunity, I have run away and come to this place—like a coward.

Here, I am no longer entangled in a web of anxieties; there are no problems pestering me every minute. My heart is strangely tranquil. I inhabit a world of idle dreams. Standing at the heart of Madhya Pradesh, surrounded by wild nature and in close proximity to the deep blue sky, I am resolved never to let numerous problems invade my mind again. I shall live my moments immersing myself in life's stream, savouring every minute of being alive, extracting all its pleasures, leaving nothing unrelished.

It is spring time! The Mahua and the Palash trees are simply luxuriating here! I want to regard the world with their infatuated eyes—what can I do about those who are driven to death by hunger, those who are senselessly killed or about the sorrows afflicting the lives of people every day, all the monstrosities—and next to all these the ghoulish glee of the rich who have captured state power by the might of money. How can I stop all this? I am tired and limp. What's the use of worrying about such problems!

It is better to remain as I am. It's past noon and I'm sitting next to a waterfall. Pieces of boulders are glittering in the sun and the air is heavy with the fragrance of countless *mahua* blossoms hanging overhead the stone mound in front of me. The underlying woods are decked out in wild blossoms shed by the palash trees. It is the order of things. The crystalline stream flows unsteadily besides the creek and breaks into frothy white spray as it dashes against rocks, here and there—a wonderous sight, this! In the distance, where the blue sky escapes my vision, I see the hazy outline of a long line of hills. I sense a deep mystery surrounding everything. I can't describe how wonderful I feel! This is the landscape of Kalidas's poem *Meghdoot*, the mythical *'Alaka'*.[1] It makes me remember the bland, innocent expression on the faces of our village women and I simultaneously recall the image of my muse—a creation of my imagination, mingling fancy with reality. I had formed different

1. The mythical 'Alaka' on the Kailas mountains has multiple meanings. It stands both for 'home' and 'place of joy,' love and plentitude; it is also a place of innocence.

mental pictures of her matching the circumstances of my life. Her image altered according to the situation I was in. At times she was a quiet, refreshing ordinary lass, at other times a flaming icon of a woman, resolutely committed to an ideal.

But the girl I see in front of me now is none of these. She isn't a figment of my imagination either. She's collecting water from the rapids. She may look like a simple rural girl, but she is different from those who have descended from the fair-complexioned Aryans—she is a tribal.

I had heard about the existence of a tribal village on the other side of the mound. Perhaps the girl comes from there. She has oil-soaked black hair with a middle parting, combed severely back and tied into a knot at the nape of her neck. Her complexion is a healthy dark brown and she has large petal-like eyes. A red and white striped saree is worn tightly around her waist. She has nothing that can attract the attention of a respectable, educated young man. Yet when I see her, for that one brief moment in the darkling, bending low and gathering water, she appears to me as perfection itself. I feel as if she is the representative of the original feminine in the wilds.

The evening deepens. The girl collects water and makes for her village. She gives a quick glance at the outlander, immaculately dressed in freshly-laundered clothes, before she leaves. There's such curiosity in that glance! She walks—I find her gait very alluring. I gaze at her as she goes ahead, taking the path down the slope and out of my vision.

What's the use of all my deliberations or my numerous considerations? Away with them—will I lose my all if I were to marry her, spend my entire life with the village folk, dancing and drinking the mahua wine? I will go there tomorrow, to their village! My whole life will pass among them where there is no scope for worry; I won't face so many difficulties. Is there anything wrong in wanting to merge my identity with theirs, live and work among them as an agricultural labourer? Man has always searched for peace in this world—won't I find it there? I will carry on my life there armed with beliefs and values of the primitive man; many of my problems would then simply disappear. Today, at this particular juncture of my life how distinctly significant the ancient adage 'ignorance is bliss' seems!

The girl is probably called Mungri, or Rangila or some other. I will till the uneven fields, below the big hill all day long and wait for her to come up the climbing road at meal times, at noon. I will get back home at dusk, dance the primitive dance with the village folk—the original dance of human beings. Piped music will be played, like it has been from times immemorial. I will become dizzy dancing to the rhythm of the village tom-toms.

Perhaps the world will dissolve in tears, she too toss and turn in sleep, the third world war engulf the world in a frenetic death dance and I remain oblivious of it all. I will stay next to the ploughed field and keep gazing at the car-borne gentlemen drive past, with eyes wide-open in amazement.

The evening darkens into night. I feel someone has painted the dark scene even darker with an invisible brush. An inky blackness has closed in all sides of the grove of shalai, sal, mahua and palash trees. Thousands of animated forest beings have come alive. A demonic light burns brightly among the shadows behind the trees, someone whispers, sounds of soft foot-fall float in, the woodland becomes suffused with suppressed laughter, the clanging of clashing cymbals come from afar.

The moon comes up—a yellow, round room. The waterfall leaps down from the mountains in glee and abandonment—thousands of little moons shine on its surface. A mild air blows in from the east. A gush of moonbeam falls and rolls over an empty space. Next to it, the tawny wood looks dark as it rubs its heap against an even darker landscape. Someone seems to have smudged the entire scene with a wet brush and rendered it a blur. The entire atmosphere is one of the land of the 'lotus eaters.' Even a wave of the hand is a redundant gesture—an irritation in a universe in meditation.

Sitting by the waterfall today, a thought enters my mind: work has no meaning: all efforts end only in hopeless defeat. An immense, unending peace exists in this environment. There is nothing for one to do in this great land of peace but rest—take a solemn rest, and contemplate nature's deep harmony with eyes half-shut.

That's it! I must go tomorrow and pin a wreath of palash flowers on the girl's hair bun. I must stay on there—the boy who had got lost has come home at last! Traversing stretches of wilderness, crossing the seven seas he has come and stands with a trembling heart at the gate of his forgotten home. Now he can with impunity ignore the raised eyebrows of those who comprise the world—I have tasted the nectar that flows through earth's woods and meadows—I want to immerse myself in it, abandoning all my senses.

Yet—I can't ignore a sneaking feeling that marrying the girl I may not be able to live happily ever after!

1949

A Fairy Tale

Rupkatha

A big car came to a halt in front of a famous newspaper office. Haranathbabu got out. He's our own Haranathbabu whose picture appears in the paper every day, in the company of the famous: Governors, politicians and the like. The reason is quite simple; he owns the newspaper and is regarded as the mogul of the newspaper world. The paper was his maiden enterprise, the fountainhead of his reputation. He had launched the project some twenty years ago. Today, getting down from the vehicle, he looked somewhat anxious.

Allow me to describe him. He is extremely fair, fat and short. One look at him tells you he suffers from high blood pressure; his face isn't pale but florid. Haranathbabu settled his dhoti pleats, asked his driver to remain where he was, and walked towards the gate swinging his head. The gatekeeper got worried. The gentleman didn't come visiting everyday, when he did, he kept the editor down to the porter on their toes. He was given to such a display of emotions—one was never sure what he would do next. He could do whatever he liked, from promoting a person to giving him the sack. He looked rather fierce today. The gatekeeper's heart went pit a pat; he had caught a whiff of alcohol when Haranathbabu went past him. The gatekeeper had no doubt that many heads would roll that day.

Haranathbabu straightaway made for the third floor of the building. Besides the editor's room, the floor contained a small cabin where a typist sat along with an errand boy who guided the visitors to the office of the editor. The boy was a new recruit—he hadn't recognized Haranath. He asked him in a patronizing manner, "What do you want?" Haranathbabu pushed him aside. He asked the typist, on his feet, to immediately leave the place. "I've some matters to discuss with the editor." Haranath entered the office making sure both had gone down. He knew no one would dare come up to the third floor so long as he was there. Reaching the ground floor, the typist heaved a sigh of relief. He had watched the mini-scuffle between the boss and the peon with eyes wide open.

The editor was sitting comfortably in his office. The window next to his seat was open. He was gazing at the other end of the park next to the building. A lot of young girls and boys had assembled there to play. The editor had been witnessing the same scene, from the open window, day after day, for the last twenty years. Children who had gathered there earlier were now powers that be, and the present lot of boys and girls were not even born then. There were few buildings or residential houses in that part of the city even some years ago; now the place had acquired an aura of respectability—houses had sprung up. The editor had seen houses coming up, one by one, and the streets getting filled up with people—in the twenty years that had fleeted past and he felt he too had changed in tune with his surroundings. He was no longer the youthful, idealistic reporter of yesteryears, but a successful, renowned man, who had won battles, and whose side whiskers had begun to gray. It's the impression he gave when one observed him at work, in office. The chair which had borne his weight over the years was on its last legs, the wall-bracket where he placed his staff still existed.

He was familiar with everything relating to the office: the scene outdoors—where rows of houses of the city touched the minaret of the blue sky with the fleecy white clouds hung scattered here and there, and the falling evening sunlight producing a wonderous sight. The broken railings of the park, the see-saws carting all the children, his office room—all were linked to his struggling years as a news reporter. He loved to see them. They were the signposts of his glorious years, the chronicle of his enterprising days.

His eyes brightened up as he mulled over his past experiences and recalled the many battles he had waged in the good old days with his total dedication to news gathering.

Blasting the door open, Haranathbabu came into his room and flew into a temper. "You ... I don't know what to do with you." Haranathbabu wasn't given to polite conversation.

The editor raised his brows as he turned to see who had forced the door open. He showed no signs of stirring at Hammathbabu's outburst. Haranath shouted again, "Have you taken leave of your senses? What kind of an editorial did you print yesterday—don't you know who the Sonarpur Cotton Mills belong to?"

The editor at last realised what all the fuss was about. He replied softly, "Oh, that edit page! Why, I had written it myself, not merely sent it to the press. But isn't it true that the mill has become a den of smugglers, a dump for contraband goods? As for the on going strike—the workers are protesting against illegal trafficking. People of this country have the right to know who are behind the shootings, the lockouts, and attempts made to break the strike with the help of those who are high up."

"Have you lost your mind? What's all this you are saying?"

The editor lowered his voice, "I have sent off another editorial piece today itself—composed more or less in the same vein." He looked out of the window. "I have written about the tyranny of the Bombay newspaper bosses, about how they are trying to silence the editors. I have written how they are obstructing our freedom of expression."

"You ..." Haranathbabu was at a loss for words. The veins in his forehead seemed about to burst.

"Idiot," he blurted out. Noticing the editor still on his chair, he shouted, "You're still sitting, not bothering to get up?"

The editor gave him a calm look. "Why don't you sit down—how long are you going to talk standing upright? Sit, sit on that chair ..." Haranathbabu had never seen anyone, from the editors down to the clerks of his office, in his long life, behave like this. He was nonplussed. "I'm sacking you, you pig ... get out." The editor was about to say something, lifting his eyes when Haranathbabu put a brake on his words and screamed, "Not another word I tell you—get out this minute!"

The editor got up slowly. He was a tall man. There wasn't a ripple of emotion on his handsome face. He took his stick and walked towards the door; he stopped for a moment and looked back. "Do I have to call the darwan?" Haranathbabu threatened. The editor latched the door, wiped his spectacles with his handkerchief and placed them back into his shirt pocket. Balancing the stick on the wall, folding his shirt sleeves and shaking the dust off them, he turned around and looked at Haranathbabu, narrowing his eyes—as if he was thinking deeply. He said calmly, taking his stick and sitting down, "You have sacked me, me who has taken your orders without a murmur for the last twenty years and today ..."

Haranathbabu was pleased at the sound of his own voice, although outwardly he appeared to fume—So the medicine had worked! The fools have to be whipped back to some order when they go beserk!—He knew the cure for unruly behaviour, he knew how to make the dunderheads work. He had had a long experience in leading the herd by the nose to get where he did.

He gave an ugly smirk, "I'm not to be blamed. You may thank your own stupidity for the predicament you are in. I've noticed you have lost your flair, your writing is sub-standard now." He giggled making his beady eyes dance. Incredible shadowy lines appeared on the side of his face, illuminated by the light of the falling sun.

The editor went on staring at him holding onto his stick he let his thumbs roll over its smooth surface. The stick was an expensive one, made out of cane. He moved close, "I want to say a few words ... maybe I won't have the opportunity ever again. I've sat on this chair for twenty precious years of my life, suffering the domination of a prodigal intellect like you. I have made up all kinds of nice stories to protect the interests of your cronies and have not published the truth. You can't imagine the inner turmoil I have undergone. All that doesn't matter anymore ... I've left that life behind." The editor came and stood at the other end of the table, Haranathbabu was taken aback.

"How's it that all of a sudden you are addressing me as 'you' rather than the formal 'thou'? Changing your tack, eh? Making a show of affection, eh?" Haranath asked, not sure he hadn't administered too harsh a dose of medicine and the remedy wasn't worse than the disease. He clearly sensed that something had gone wrong; but was far from guessing what it could be. He comforted himself by the thought that once his ravings subsided, the editor, aware of the hardships in store, was bound to change his tune. However, that was another matter. Right now, Haranath didn't feel too comfortable about being alone in a room, face to face, with a subordinate talking back to him. It was beyond his powers of endurance.

The cane came thrashing on his face catching him unawares. Haranathbabu leapt up with alacrity, the next moment he slumped into his chair. The thrashing continued—a dark curtain draped his vision. He saw pyrotectonics—a strange sight! Haranathbabu could hardly swallow the fact that he was getting soundly flogged—Giving a small scream he stared at the editor, his eyes wide open in fright. His head began to spin. After a few more lashes the editor stopped. Haranath reclined against the table, blood was oozing from the wounds on his face and his arms; it took him some moments to regain his composure.

The editor drew heavy breaths, the exertion—exhibiting such prowess with his two hands—was a bit too much at his old age. He wiped perspiration off his forehead, as Haranathbabu leaned across the table and tried to reach for the telephone. All of a sudden his hand was whipped. For the first time in his life Haranath folded his palms. The speed with which he accomplished it was hard to believe.

The editor began to give a lecture now. He spoke out in a cracked voice:

"I have had to print your picture—you fat lump—day after day, ignoring important news items." The editor had assumed an air of delivering a scholarly disquisition. "That's why I have had to send off those editorials, one by one. I wanted the people to get a glimpse of what was going on behind the invisible censorship wrought by your mighty arms." The editor was beginning to look ugly, resembling a fierce tiger about to pounce on it's prey. His two eyes blazed furiously, his chest heaved and the nostrils of his sharp nose flared. All of this was anathema to Haranath.

"What haven't I done for you—I have done so many contemptible things because I had to. But last night I faced utter ruin and you are responsible for that—you know that?" The editor now bent forward and clutched a bunch of Haranath's neatly coiffed hair in his fists. Haranath gaped at him, feeling as if he were contemplating the water that had escaped from the breach on the dam of the river Padma, and was streaming everywhere. He sat open-mouthed, not looking a bit like the well-dressed gentleman we had become familiar with, from the newspaper columns.

The editor let go of him and stood straight up. His gaze returned to the scene outside the window. The children were still playing, there were no lack of people on the streets.

Suddenly Haranath was on his hands and knees; he fell on the editor's feet. Haranathbabu was adept at crouching down at people's feet. He had had a long practice in it and was able to accomplish the feat with aplomb. But it is also true that pulled up by the hair, one can't help making that gesture. The editor dragged him and flung him back on the chair. Haranathbabu noticed that the quiet, soft spoken reporter was beginning to look dangerous. His gums had started to bleed, and an ugly black mark appeared over one of his eyes. He thought he would make one last attempt at peace. He said "Brother, forget all that I've done in a fit of temper; after all one can only pressurise those one loves." The editor's response was quick. "Shut up—you are the worst of them all—the criminals, the cause of my destruction. She died last night. She was carrying a child. She had suffered so much pain all her life; she put up with everything for my sake!" The editor spoke in a frosty voice.

"Why not go on leave—for a few days? Take a holiday, you'll feel better. I know your wife was a saint." Haranathbabu spoke in hurried tones jerking sideways. The editor continued to look at him, appearing unnaturally calm. Haranath felt uneasy. He got up on his unsteady feet and tried to lend a poignant aspect to his lacerated face. The cane flew making a cutting noise that reverberated in the entire room. The editor had resumed his ferocious attack, gasping and repeating in a broken voice, "Vampire—this is for forcing me to keep my mouth shut and this—this is how your servant pays you back!" Haranathbabu tried in vain to ward off the blows; the editor with enough physical strength in his tall frame pulled out all the stops. Finally, Haranath burst into tears, he wept like a helpless child, his anger bore no result. He fell on his side moaning faintly at every fresh blow—even that ceased after a while. The editor flogged Haranathbabu at random, oblivious of his surroundings.

The group of officers that had assembled on the first and second floors of the building waited anxiously.

The editor couldn't deliver the ultimate blow, the cane broke into pieces on the arm of the chair and made a racket.

Is Haranathbabu worth the price of such a fine specimen of a bamboo cane? Oh! What has the editor gone and done!

At last the editor recovered his senses. He was extremely exhausted, carried away by emotion he had outstepped his bounds. He threw away the pieces of cane which, rotating a few times, made half a circle and came to rest on the ground.

Haranathbabu had already passed out. Streams of blood from his body slowly flowed on to the chair, and trickled in drops to the floor. They formed little rivulets and travelled in the direction of the rain pipes. A lot of blood flowed. Perhaps all that was for the better, it might alleviate Haranath's blood pressure problems! The editor wiped his face with his trembling hands, neatly unrolled his shirt sleeves, patted his hair and gazed at the inert body sprawled flat on his face on the table.

He went out, bolting the door from the outside. Blood kept streaming out. The dying sun brightened up the silent room in the lustrous red colour of the hibiscus flowers. The broken bits of the cane lay abandoned on the floor.

The editor went down the stairs. The driver watched his retreating figure and wondered how long it would take for his boss to reappear—he had to take him somewhere else. Inside the press there was a huge tumult. Another person had joined the ever-expanding band of men; another soldier was added to the resistance army.

1948

Raja

All of a sudden it poured, at a most inconvenient moment. Raja was about to go out on a business trip; now he couldn't. It was no ordinary drizzle; it was raining cats and dogs. Piles of water fell like thick ropes and obscured the scene all around. It flowed down the rain pipe at a high velocity and spattered in all directions. Raja retreated from the front door making an ugly grimace—*'Sha-a-la!'* he blurted out.

Raja was a poet. He was a pickpocket too. In other words, he was both these things at once. This might seem strange, but not impossible. He was not only a poet, but an afficionado of poetry as well. The subject-matter of his poetry was entirely new. Apart from being a pickpocket, he was a drunkard; one was not sure whether he picked people's pockets to get money for booze, or whether he got drunk because he had money to blow.

Everybody has a past; when the past has some distinction it acquires the contours of history. Raja had an ordinary past; he was impoverished in that respect. The son of a gentleman, he had given up studies when he was studying for a BA degree. He discovered that studies were not getting him anywhere, and what he wanted was to make lots of money. He struck his name off the college rolls. His parents had died sometime ago; he didn't feel responsible for anyone. He sold the house he inherited, pocketed the money and set out to find a place for himself in the wide world. For the time being, Calcutta was the entire universe to him.

What followed is rather simple—he was a poet and wanted to experience life. He had come to believe that alcohol, hotel rooms and prostitutes were what constituted life. It didn't take him long to gather suitable companions—Raja began to savour our kind of life: home-brewed liquor soon replaced foreign spirits—he learnt the easiest way to manage. By this time, the old Raja, of his college days, had taken a back seat and another Raja with long, deft fingers had begun his era. This is how one can sum up the events of the past five years.

The tension between Raja's two selves to possess his soul, like the sun and the moon vying with each other for a place in the sky, had been resolved long since. But Raja continued to be fond of poetry. He would recite from Auden, Spenser, Lawrence, Pound and Eliot whenever he became sozzled. In a nutshell, this then was the Raja we knew.

The early morning's torrential rain made Raja irritated. It was almost half past eight and he had to catch the tram car plying in the main street. The office crowd would begin to thin again after ten. But Raja didn't relish the idea of going about the commercial hub of the city soaked to the skin. He was fed up—fucking rain, he muttered to himself.

No—there were no signs of the rain abating—outside there was a continuous downpour—a knee deep water had already collected in the streets. Empty cars swished past making a commotion in the flood and creating huge ripples on the surface of the water. The flowing drains on the side lanes spilled all over with muck. A drenched crow, perched on the cornice of the third floor of Mallickbabu's house made a flapping sound. It too was unhappy!

Raja lay, half-reclined, on the mat with his eyes partly-shut. He had been out carousing till one in the morning, the night before, and his body felt limp. He felt nice about continuing to lie, as if he was in a stupor, and listening to the dreamy drone of the falling rain. He gave a yawn. Almost immediately he sat bolt upright and wandered how much time had passed. He looked at the clock—it was a few minutes past ten! He fell into a foul mood—nothing pleased him.

Then the sky cleared, the water level of the street came down, and people went out into the open. The roads were still thick with slime. Raja's eyes burned. He splashed some water on his eyes and his face and ran a comb through his hair. Suddenly, the door latch rattled loudly. Raja opened the door—a postman pressed a letter in his hand and left.

How extraordinary! A letter no less—a fat envelope with his name written on it in an elegant, sophisticated hand. He wondered what it was all about. There wasn't any point in going out now—he reckoned. He went back to his room, slightly afraid. Receiving a letter was not a part of his normal routine—who would want to write to him?

He forcibly tore the envelope open. It was an invitation: golden letters printed against the background of a bluish paper—

an invitation sent by 'Bahni Chakra' to attend the circle's annual get together on the following day. It had yesterday's date—a little note in long hand was appended at the back of the card:

I don't know whether this card will reach you—
do come if you get the message. I wait for you,
full of expectation, Sunil

'Bahni Chakra'—a club he had founded along with his college companions and eight others! Memories flooded his mind. Its very name resonated with hundreds of little hopes and desires of the past days! He had conferred the name to the association; his friend Buddha had painted the sign-board. They had gathered in Sunil's room to discuss the world or simply to chat. So many meetings, festivities had taken place in that little room! They had got hold of singers and literary figures from Calcutta and had brought them over to that place. They had feverishly gone about collecting funds in the hot afternoon sun, had pasted posters on the city walls in the middle of the night, carrying ladders on their shoulders.

'Bahni Chakra'—the very name brought back the image of his entire college life—the golden days of his youth—the cricket fields, the debating society, the social and literary get togethers. Girls! Gauri, Snigdha, Maya and one other—he couldn't remember the name—knew her by her roll number sixty seven—was it? Images of those college girls, standing in a row, as also Buddha, Sunil, Ananda and Bimal, his college mates, came alive in his mind's eye. He knew those girls and boys would never disappear from his mental horizon, become old or die. They would always remain vivacious in his thoughts. The flaming red wheels, painted on the signboard of 'Bahni chakra', were spinning at great speed; the half-concealed figure of the Sun god, mounted on an eighty-seven-horse driven chariot, holding reins in one hand and a dagger in the other, was smiling down at him from the brink of the distant Udaigiri rills—Raja's life was again in contact with the stuff of history!

But how could the boys find his address? No one had an inkling about his present den. He looked at the signature in the card once more. Sunil! So he was still the secretary of the club! His friends had not abandoned the circle—but how could they get hold of his address—it was puzzling.

It wasn't important—they had called, had asked him to attend a meeting of the club. He would go, no matter what—Sunil, Buddha and all his college friends had asked him to come! Their message carried the fragrance of the bygone days, tinged with tears, quarrels and laughter—Yes, he would go, certainly.

Could he go? Raja gazed at the reflection of his face in the mirror. The past five years of his life had pushed his eyes into deep, dark sockets, his eyeballs blazed as in some beasts of prey, ugly lines appeared on either corners of his mouth, blackish gums and broken teeth peeped in-between his discoloured, tartar coated lips when he smiled. His hair had grown long and wasn't oiled—should he go?

Besides he wasn't sure his friends were the same—that weighed down by worldly cares they had remained as dynamic as before. Perhaps he would find them totally changed, lacking in the innocent exuberance they once had. But their picture remained unaltered in his mind; Raja had preserved their youthful image even to this day.

Disappointed, he uncorked a bottle at noon. It was the only medicine he could think of to rid his mind of all doubts and uncertainties. Emotion welled up inside his heart, his demented brain began to pound, his chin quivered, he felt like throwing up; drunk, he began to weep. But he was resolute about his decision. He would take the morning train, reach them in the afternoon, get back the next morning. It was only a matter of a few hours.

Raja got off the train at a small mofussil town late afternoon. There were low, fleeting clouds in the sky. It had drizzled a little. He felt he was being given a big welcome as he came and stood in front of the familiar staircase of the old building. The air was friendly—the freshly washed green trees, the tall wet grass and the damp earth combined to exude a scent that reverberated in his entire being. He had missed this jumble of smell for such a long time! Strangely, he wasn't irritated by the muck around his feet—

He walked, feeling happy. He had spent the entire afternoon on the train, sitting by the window and looking out. He had been thrilled by a dream he had when he dozed off during the early hours of the journey. He had dreamt he had gone back to his former life—he was a second-year student all over again.

He saw his mother, clear as a picture, calling out to him, serving the rice.

"Khoka, o Khoka! Come at once! How long am I to wait with the food?"

He saw himself bursting into the room. "What is it, dear old Ma? Ah yes! Say that—what's the fish, Hilsa? Good! Ma, serve me quick, it's getting late."

Ma sat with a hand fan cooling the warm rice. She said, "Will you get back a little early today, Baba?"

He got suspicious. He was used to being scolded; her endearing voice made him feel rather uncomfortable. He asked softly, "What's the matter?"

"Its *shasti* tomorrow—you have to buy me some fruit in the afternoon, what else?" she looked the other way.

Raja gulped down some water, threw the glass on the floor and got up in a huff.

"I knew it—it won't do I tell you—get someone else to do the shopping; I have a game to play.

He wanted to run, bunk the scene completely. Ma said, "You little monkey—you haven't even tasted the *ambal*!"

"Place some here"—Raja stuck out his palm. Then his mother's smiling face got lost in the streams of smoke of the running train. Raja woke up. His eyes were wet, perspiration hung on his body. He couldn't sleep anymore.

Ma had died of asthmatic fever soon afterwards; she hadn't received proper treatment. It was she who had, singly, kept the family together, managing the work of ten people so long as she was alive. She was an ordinary mother, like everybody else's. Raja thought a person like his mother could never die. In his mind she was forever living, putting up with all his waywardness, comforting him in sorrow.

Why only his mother—his relatives of those days, appeared bright and alive in his mind's eye. They could never die. His friends remained youthful, holding on to their adolescent impetuosity. That was how it was going to be—as long as I am alive—Raja said quietly to himself.

The old familiar environment, the little acts of living, he had been witness to day after day, now filled him with an immense joy. The sun, leaping out suddenly from behind the clouds, shone fiercely—the moisture on the grass and the leaves began to glisten—and Raja remembered how he had loved the monsoon season, how he had exulted in an inexplicable joy at the appearance of the clouds, how the poetry of Kalidasa and Rabindranath Tagore, celebrating the rains, had sent him into a frenzy. Strange that he now lived forgetting the joys he had once experienced. This town was his proper place, his favourite haunt. He knew it like the palm of his hand. See there—that's the sitting room of Banamali Kaviraj, and next to it the rows of houses of the people of the locality. Gouri lived in that tall, three-storied building—did she still live there? He wondered. Gouri was a fellow-student. Quiet, and reserved, a fair-complexioned girl with light brown eyes not beautiful by any stretch of imagination. But somehow he had found her graceful. The shy voice of that comely, slightly built girl had sounded sweet as honey to his ears. There might not have been anything between them—really, but thanks to the exertions of the college wall poets their names had got linked and rumours of their friendship spread far and wide. His liking for her probably had no meaning; nevertheless she appeared in his thoughts, to this day, whenever he contemplated untainted innocence. 'How is she? Where is she now?' 'Let her remain happy and well, innocent Gauri—may she live long in prosperity'—Raja wished, deeply moved.

Raja came upon his old locality where the road curved. He saw his house, the one he had sold before he left; he went past it. A little child was playing in the courtyard. A young boy was encouraging a twelve or thirteen year-old to steal guava fruit from a tree in the corner of the square. It was *their* guava tree—

now his existence was wiped out of the place. The house had new habitants, revealed new faces. The evening lights came on in the street. Sunil's house stood at the mouth of the main road; a strip of brightness fell obliquely upon it—sounds of boisterous laughter waved out of the interior of the house and shook the earth.

Raja had gone about the whole afternoon in muck and slime. He was giving his old town a look over. He saw countless familiar faces, shook hands with many persons. He came up the stairs and straightaway entered the room now. He noticed the old carpet, the ancient signboard still stuck on the wall—bright though the colours had faded. A poem by him with the date of the inception of 'Bahni Chakra' was pasted on top of the doorway. Sunil was there as also Ananda, Buddha was huddled in one corner. Bimal sat in the middle of the carpet with Choto Khoka next to him. There were others—Amar, Prabin, and Jiten. Raja gazed at them—one by one—standing at the door. 'No they hadn't changed that much.'

The next moment a commotion rented the sky—the welcoming tones of high-pitched voices of a group of eight boys at the unexpected arrival of their long-lost buddy.

"Who is it—Raja, no less!"

"Today the beloved has come back into our fold."

"Hurrah! Let's go for a row—Raja is here!"

"How wonderful! *Colin Clouts come home again*."[1]

"Sit here—O *Mary go and put the kettle on*—a little tea is indicated."

---

1 'Edmund Spenser.

"So Raja you have received our letter!"

"Raja, I've composed a new poem—you must listen to it."

It was Buddhadev who realised things were getting out of hand. "Stop it—all of you, he's just got off the train—give him some time to recover."

Raja rested a while, listened to Amar recite his poem, heard Ananda talk about his health. Ananda loved to eat; chronic dyspepsia couldn't stop him from stuffing himself—Jiten had become a deputy magistrate, Choto Khoka, a professor—Ananda's business was roaring. Amar practiced law in the town; Sunil was the secretary of the Student's Union; he had become quite famous. Buddha was a budding commercial artist and doing extremely well. He heard about the others—all were earning their living, scattered in different parts of the country. He also had Gauri's news—she had got married.

Raja sat, resting against a cushion, his eyes shut. He couldn't believe he was there—actually— in the old sitting room, among old friends—it was a dream! Buddha and Amar, sitting in the corner, picked up a quarrel. Raja felt like laughing. Nothing had changed—those two had fought like this every day in the past. Raja was so used to watching Buddha tease Amar about his poetry—they were the same as before! Sunil told him every year they had assembled at that place on that day no matter where they were—the eight of them—no other person. But they hadn't had any news of where he was.

Opening his eyes, Raja asked,

"But, where did you get my address?"

"What's so strange in that? Didn't you come across my elder brother somewhere a few days ago?"

Raja remembered a chance meeting in the tram; it had lasted a couple of minutes. Sarojda had probably asked for his address. Raja couldn't think why he had told him the truth—that was a month ago—the gentleman hadn't forgotten.

"Let go of all that," Sunil added, "Tell us what all you've been doing—you were the cleverest among us all!"

Raja began to churn up a mound of lies. Soon he was enjoying every bit of the beautiful story he had concocted. He was a mining officer of a state in Madhya Pradesh. His salary was adequate; he was given free living quarters, enjoyed all kinds of perks. Yes ... he had married—rather suddenly. There was no time to inform friends. He had a child, who he called Munna; his wife called him khokon. No, he hadn't found a 'proper name' for him, as yet. His wife?—oh yes, she was quite pretty. They were living 'happily ever after' etc. He had come to Calcutta taking two months leave from office. Of course he would bring his wife over there—only after some time. He was visiting his in-laws tomorrow—had a wedding to attend. Raja went on and on—The Raja of 'Bahni Chakra,' a student leader and the object of love and adulation of the friends he was seeing after such a long time. Then there were songs, and laughter, the drumming of the tabla and the pleasing notes of the harmonium. The night deepened and they were called to dinner. The nine of them made a huge racket, sitting on the floor in a row, and eating. Raja ate happily after ages.

Ananda and Buddha left at night—the three that remained fell on the carpet and went off to sleep. Sunil turned the lights off and went indoors.

Life was sweet, unimaginably sweet! The misfortunes agreeable. The past joys had lost none of its appeal. To Raja, sitting by himself, heaving deep sighs for no rhyme or reason was happiness itself. Reading about others travelling to strange parts of the world he himself had never visited, was enjoyable.

He too would embark on a new journey—he would give up alcohol, cast aside his evil companions, never again return to Calcutta—he would stay there—only at that place—wouldn't he find a job for himself in the town? His mother, Gauri, Buddha, and the shy looks of the new Professor of English floated in his mind's eye—Ma, Gauri, Ananda, the college, the pot-bellied Principal of the College; Gauri, Ma—the images became increasingly blurred. The atmosphere became foggy—the grass gave off a nice smell. The yellow moon, hurrying far, peeped in-between the rain-laden clouds. The hills of Ramgiri came to his mind, with a skeleton like figure with only a scarf on, standing with his arms outstretched—his hair billowing in the wind, a pair of broken golden armlets clasped around his wrists—he was

> *A certain Yaksha who deprived of greatness and exiled for one year, because he had neglected to do his duty was extremely unhappy at being separated from his wife and had taken refuge in the hills of Ramgiri where water hallowed by Janak's daughter, flowed among the shaded trees*[2].

Raja felt that Yaksha had now passed beyond his cursed existence and was flying high into that blessed abode where all his desires would come to rest; where he would be reinstalled in full self-esteem in the place of everlasting beauty and peace.

---

2. *Meghdootam verse one,* Yaksha is passion-ridden *(Kami)* and self-willed and is tied to his place of expiation, Ramgiri, by the terms of the curse.

He turned on his side. Buddha was snoring in sleep. His train departed at 5:30 am. Sunil woke him up at half past four—the time of unalloyed peace, the moment of prayer and devotion to the Eternal One—Raja drew deep breaths.

The air was fresh, the sky though overcast hadn't given way to rain. Raja got up to clean his teeth.

Sunil's mother was up at night to prepare tea and snacks; she was sitting and waiting for him now, displaying motherly concern. Raja sat chatting with her for a while—he felt happy. He had spent only a few hours in their company but already his cup of happiness was overflowing. He knew he would have to get back.

It was time to leave. Raja went to the sitting room and began to put on his clothes; Buddha and the others were still asleep—they looked so tired—he didn't want to wake them up. Slipping the banian over his head he thought about visiting them again. He would return—'I will be back'—he repeated to himself, over and over again.

Raja couldn't find his *kurta*, perhaps it lay buried under the mound of clothes on the rack. He kept looking for it. Sunil came with the request that he should delay his departure for a few minutes. Mashima had *amsatta* for him; Sunil would go and bring it, then take him to the station. There was his kurta—tucked away beneath the blue shirt! Something rolled out of its pocket as Raja lifted the shirt—a purse, heavy with stuff! Raja's thin, long, dexterous fingers began to tingle. Before he knew it, he had lifted the purse from the floor; his heart shook a bit as he gave a quick glance at his sleeping companions out of the corner of his eye—he opened the wallet. There were wads of bank notes in it—the purse must belong to Ananda and money must have come from his business deals. Raja quickly pushed the wallet back into the shirt pocket. He put his kurta on.

He felt dizzy, his voice had become thick—with one stroke he had wiped out his past—his balmy past!

Coils of heavy mist rose upwards. The charioteer of 'Bahni Chakra,' the Sun god, who held reins in one hand, had a half-raised whip in the other now. His eyes still danced in mirth, his face was still radiant in smile but a filthy fog was swiftly snaking its way up his broad front, rising higher and higher, slowly obscuring the face of the benevolent deity. Ma, Gauri—Ma, Meghdoot, Ananda—all disappeared behind the veil of the fog. Raja raised his hands and tried to remove the murky shadows.

Sunil called out to him from the front gate—it was time for the train. He was holding a piece of *amsatta* wrapped in a fine cloth in his hands.

"Come on Raja, no more dilly-dallying if you want to catch the train. We must be off now!"

"I'm coming," Raja had recovered his senses. He gulped—gave Ananda a wary glance and picked up the wallet from the shirt pocket with his nimble, delicate and artistic fingers.

1948

Touchstone

Paraspathar

Banarasilal had come upon him in a coal mining town, deep in the wilderness of Madhya Pradesh. As a singer, he had been many times on the road, visited all kinds of places, and encountered different types of people, but he hadn't met anyone quite like him. He mused about the extraordinary large eyes of the time-keeper Chandrakanta, whenever he sat by himself in a quiet corner of his room, with no work in hand. Today, he thought about him all over again because of a person he had met in the street. Somehow those eyes of Chandrakanta's had given a dream-like glow to some remarkable days of his life—detached from the obscurity of his past—those were the days of his youth, when he had a bounce in his step, soul in his singing, and love in his heart.

A valley rested on the edges of what was once the Vindhya forest of ancient India. The place had lost none of its primitive grandeur. A small human habitation had sprung up there beside a thin mountain stream owing to the presence of a coal mine in its vicinity. The inclinations, the local passenger trains, the rail yard, rows of wagons, the time office or the blackish coal dust hadn't succeeded in destroying the beauty of the ancient woods or its modern western type bungalows; even the mud hutments of the miners had acquired a pristine appeal from the neighbouring lofty, yellowish mountains and the vast stretches of rugged, ochre-coloured plain land.

Banarasilal had gone there on an invitation to sing during the Holi festival. He had to perform at a local institute. He was overwhelmed by the charm of the place and the house of the Chief engineer where he had to stay. The bungalow, enclosed on all sides by a white wall, had a rugged grassland at its back which stretched exceedingly far. Trees stood here and there and the road in the front, encircling the Jharsi hill, went all the way up.

Banarasilal was not an ordinary singer—he had a genuine aesthetic sense—he was educated. In his youth he had painted pictures, and because he belonged to the class of modern classical musicians, he was Catholic in his taste. He had liked the place so much that he expressed his wish to spend some more time there—a few extra days. He was delighted at the thought of resting some time from his extremely busy schedule and whiling them away in this secluded cradle among the virgin peaks.

He sang at the Institute on his very first night—the full-moon night of Holi. He began with a song in the *Kafi raga*:

Oh! What happiness is in store for us today, what happiness! The lord is playing holi with us!

As he repeated the opening lines, over and over again, he became immersed in the emotion-filled prelude to the lyric. Mohammed Jan stroked the tabla, Monoharprasad strummed away the sarengi at his back, while Banarasilal sang, gently pulling at the tanpura strings. The engineer had settled himself in one side of the hall; rows of audience sat on the other side. The light was dim and the back-end of the room was plunged in darkness. The world outside, however, was bathed in a splendid radiance. The spring moon had cast an enchanting spell over entire nature, animate and inanimate, and had invested the silent undulating land, reaching out to the distant horizon, with mystery.

Banarasilal kept on singing, preserving the purity of the classical style, gesturing with his hands and rolling his head.

He didn't remember how long he sang; the singing came to an end after a while—the tabla ceased to make rhythmical patterns, the sarengi went silent. But the singing had already lost its charm once he had stopped composing the notes of *Kafi* and had taken up *raga Kedara* on audience request. He was no longer inspired and couldn't suffuse his song with feelings; the *madhyam* in the scale simply failed to resonate.

While he was exchanging a few words with his audience at the end of his performance, Banarasilal had noticed a man get up from the corner and leave. The man had been sitting motionless as a pillar throughout. But Banarasilal had seen him becoming restless when he had moved on to *raga Kedara*. The man looked ordinary, with a khaki shirt and a pair of khaki half-pants on. Nevertheless, Banarasilal had a hunch he was a connoisseur. The Chief engineer, who had been sitting quietly watching Banarasilal sing, cleared his throat now and gave a smile. Banarasilal had been singing to the crowd, he was no longer enthusiastic. The twists and turns of the tabla continued to produce intricate *bols*, his own voice moved up and down the musical scale, the audience responded with a thunderous applause, but Banarsilal felt something vital was missing.

The musical soiree ended late at night when the moon had already climbed to the middle of the sky, and the fairyland edged by mountains had sunk into a deep sleep, making the Changbhakar mountain range in the distance scarcely visible. As Banarasilal walked home he saw a man come forward where the road curved; it was the same person who had got up and left the hall minutes ago. He came near and greeted him with folded palms.

"Namaste, Ostadji! I hear you are staying on a few more days ... can I come and see you tomorrow afternoon, if you can spare me some time? I'm longing to hear you sing *Kafi* again!" He was looking straight at Banarasilal. In the darkness of the night the man's eyes appeared calm but they were glittering brightly and were quite remarkable.

"Surely..." Banarasilal replied. "Come tomorrow afternoon, if you must. To give pleasure is my sole mission in life!"

The man bade him goodbye with his head down and slowly walked down the slope. The Chief engineer roared with laughter as soon he went out of their sight. "What's the matter?" Banarasilal asked. "You have fallen under his spell—I see—he can make things hot for you. The chap is a time keeper, in charge of the attendance register of the mine, but totally insane—sings, talks nonsense most of the time—people here don't give him a damn; that's why he latches onto any new person he comes across," the engineer said.

"He wanted to hear me sing again—I hope you don't mind his coming over." Banarasilal said, walking.

"Not at all... how can you even think like that, Ostadji!"

The conversation ending on that note, the two walked home in silence.

MohammedJan tabalchi and Monoharprasadji went away the very next day, only Banarasilal and his tanpura were left behind. Visitors called on him at the break of dawn as the Chief engineer went to work. Soon the morning came to an end, the day rolled in, and the callers began to leave. The Chief engineer too departed after an afternoon meal. Left to himself, fighting sleep, Banarasilal wondered when the man would turn up.

After a while he heard someone cough behind the door—it was him! The man had come in quietly, removing his red earthen-coloured canvas shoes. Banarasilal had a good look at him for the first time in broad day light. The man's eyes were really astonishing—so large and protuberant!

The man greeted him with a shy smile. "Sir, I've come to hear you sing as you had promised yesterday. My name is Chandrakanta Sarkar. I work here as a clerk. I couldn't come in the morning as I had to report to work."

"Come on in," Banarasilal said aloud, "'Let's talk for a while, shall we? I'll take up singing afterwards. What do you say?"

Sitting in one corner of the carpet the man looked grateful. "Couldn't we practice music now, if you don't mind? What's there to talk about?" he said.

"Why should I mind? I'll begin with the *alap* straightaway. A song simply won't take off without the tabla. Besides... the *alap*, the prelude to the song, contains the essence of the *raga*—so here I go!" Banarasilal began to sing pulling at his tanpura strings and soon the room became suffused with the melodious notes of *Kafi*. Banarasilal was himself totally overcome by the sacred feeling the music evoked.

Moments passed. Registering the concluding note Banarasilal opened his half-shut eyes. He saw Chandrakanta sitting quietly, his face buried in his soiled khaki half-pants. Breaking the silence of the room, Chandrakanta now asked, "Doesn't music awaken strange thoughts in you?"

"What exactly do you mean?" Banarasilal said.

"For instance, so many images flitted across my mind when I heard you sing. A musical note, even the sound of a conch shell produces pictures in my mind's eye. Do you understand what I mean? It's so difficult..."

Chandrakanta gulped and went silent. All of a sudden he leaned forward and said excitedly, "I can't express my thoughts clearly, you know... It's a matter of feeling. Take for instance—the experience I have of all the rituals, the dance of the lights, incense burning, whenever I hear the sound of the conch shell, or the ringing of the temple bell," he went on gesturing and talking while Banarasilal listened with rapt attention. Finally, he uttered a few words in quiet agreement. "Yes, I do understand. It's not at all strange to have those sensations when you listen to music, lost to the world.

Chandrakanta appeared delighted. "So, you do think it's possible, don't you?" He laughed heartedly. "I had tried to explain this to someone one day and as a result people started to give me strange looks." Chandrakanta laughed as if there were nothing in the world as funny; he was in stitches, with his head tilted on one side and his eyes glittering strangely among the peculiar folding of his skin.

All of a sudden he was serious. "Music is greater than painting," he proclaimed loudly. "It does man good... besides it's absolutely indefensible to gossip about others. Music keeps man alive. You've noticed how children fall asleep to music, how we are at peace with ourselves listening to it. At times when a note reaches a crescendo you go into raptures. Music plays on the mind, it also affects our bodies. That has been my experience. I mean..." He broke off abruptly; stealing a glance at Banarasilal he lowered his eyes. But Banarsilal had seen in that brief glance the merciless look of a mad man.

Chandrakanta grinned revealing his gums. "Doesn't matter... we'll talk about all that later. I must go now." He spoke rapidly as he went out of the room with his head down. He left after putting on his shoes and giving Banarasilal a humble salute. Banarasilal kept on sitting, his attention directed on the man.

The next day Chandrakanta came along with a host of Banarasilal's admirers and sat in his room. It was almost three in the afternoon when the Chief engineer suggested they go on a tour of the place. Chandrakanta accompanied them. The tour made a deep impression on Banarasilal. He remembers till this day the appearance of the dip pit in the bowels of the earth, the jet-black coals, the fan room at the mouth of the main inclination, the attendance room, and the loco line. A current of cold air was blowing in the place.

As the group walked ahead, Banarasilal saw water seeping from the crevices of the walls, a network of little tunnels emerging here and there from a big one, miners at work and wagons loaded with men moving outside and returning—all amidst pitch darkness. The walls on either side of the cave were so black in colour that Banarasilal felt he was sitting in the dark with his eyes shut. At last they reached the spot where work was in progress. Holes were being dug in the embankment with the help of a poorly lit safety lamp in preposterous obscurity. The cracks on the walls caused by the stroke of the axe glinted in the faint light. To Banarasilal everything appeared fantastic!

Then came the explosion. The pit soon got filled with gun-powder smoke and he along with others moved away from the spot through countless tunnels. Only one man stayed behind to light the wick. A little later he heard six thudding sounds, one after the other. The walls of the embankment began to shake at intervals and the ground under their feet became strangely alive. The noise echoing all over melted away after some time. Banarasilal and the engineer went back to inspect the place. Big chunks of coal lay in piles. There was a huge indentation on the surface of the embankment. Someone called out to them from behind. It was Chandrakanta. "Ostadji have you enjoyed the experience?" he asked, "I for one love to witness the demolition work. The sound of the cartridges going off is also so attractive. Besides it's the human beings who are savouring the history of their livelihood in the bowels of the earth, aren't they?" The coolies were splitting the coal with their axes and hauling them up. Regarding them, Banarasilal uttered gravely, "Ah, yes!" Chandrakanta was overjoyed.

"I feel thrilled to bits when the ground trembles under the impact of the walls caving in and a low rumbling sound permeates everywhere," he exclaimed. Banarasilal observed Chandrakanta's face in the dark. His eyes were gleaming like glow worms in the soft light of the lamp. He felt there was something terribly strange about them. The way he stealthily moved or his hushed voice—all appeared peculiar to him, standing underground, in the dark, silent tunnel.

The engineer called out, "Let's go back now, you've seen all that there is ... Chandrakanta Babu will you come along with us?"

"Why not, Sir."

They came out into the open and were dazed by the brightness outside.

The engineer repeated, "Chandrakanta, take Ostadji along with you. I have to get back to work."

"Very well, Sir." Chandrakanta replied.

It was early afternoon. The two of them reached the top of the mine, surmounting the difficulties of ascending the rugged slope. They were both keen about making it to the other side of the pit. Chandrakanta said. "Are you busy now?"

"No, why do you ask?"

"Then we can take a stroll around the place ... that's all. Have you seen the waterfall in the Khongapani hills, where coal was first discovered?"

"Don't think I have."

"It's a must for all visitors; the place is inscribed with beauty and history. A Polish prospector, fagged out travelling, had once sought refuge in the place; then by chance he discovered layers of coal. Soon afterwards he located the perimeters of a coal mine in the neighbourhood." They were still walking. Banarasilal was getting curiouser and curiouser about the strange man.

"But you haven't told me your story," he said.

"My story? It's so ordinary ... I belong to a village in the Comilla district. I was working as a teacher in a local school after completing my teacher's training. Suddenly I had a whim and left the job and came to Begumpat in Secunderbad to work for a construction company. I was good at my job, but after an incident I gave that up. I finally landed here, two years ago, after scouring all kinds of places for work."

Banarasilal was interested in how he made his ends meet. He asked, "Tell me how much salary do you get."

"About rupees fifteen a week."

"Can you get by with that amount?"

"I live alone—there's no reason not to—besides how much do you think one needs to live in this place? The company gives us a place to stay—the mess bill adds up to rupees twenty-five a month. I don't bother about what I wear. I'm not interested in clothes. I have two sets of khaki half-pants and shirts. I wash one, wear one. I wear a lunghi when I'm at home—that's about it."

"Then you manage to save some ... what do you do with the money put away?"

"I don't have any dependents, I put the money into a post office savings account."

Banarasilal had an idea: "To travel home, I suspect," he interjected.

Chandrakanta started up, and was about to say something. He made an inaudible sound and looked away.

The mountain in front of them sloped towards a plateau and the Jharsi hill appeared in the distance. Mud huts with thatched roofs lined the path which lay in the middle. People were assembled there—some labourers—one could see a few women among them. Seeing them approach the place, a tall, well-built man ran up to them. He saluted Chandrakanta and said, "Matadin has been bitten by the krait snake." Both of them were taken aback. Chandrakanta rushed to the place, Banarasilal followed him. The crowd of people moved to the side to allow them in. A hindusthani labourer was lying senseless on the ground, frothing at the mouth; his body showed every sign of being infected by the snake's venom. An old woman was sitting next to the body beating her chest and groaning softly. She became jittery seeing them approach. The man had been stung by a snake while he was working in the field. Someone had dragged him there and left without administering any anodyne.

The snake had bitten the man's toenail. Chandrakanta sat on his knees to inspect the wound. He stretched his hand for a piece of cloth without lifting his eyes. A person prepared to dart towards the mud hutments, but the woman had already torn a portion of her tattered saree and given it to him. The old woman had become unusually quiet. She was sitting motionless.

Chandrakanta made several bandages out of the cloth, and tied them tightly around the labourer's arms. He gazed at him strangely, patted him all over affectionately. His lips were moving rapidly as he said something in a low, sing-song voice. Suddenly noticing so many eyes riveted on him he got up with alacrity.

"I've done all I can," he said, "it would be better if you took him to the hospital now. He'll get proper treatment there. There's nothing to worry, he'll recover for sure.

The men carried away the body while the woman kept sitting as before. Banarasilal and others also prepared to leave. They had gone a few steps when Chandrakanta went back to the woman and said, "Maiji ... he's going to live, don't worry. I'm telling you he'll recover soon." The woman raised her sad eyes and said, "Live long, dear boy. Lord bless you!" Who knew what she found in Chandrakanta's face to give her this hope!

Soon they were back in the interior of the forest. All around them stood the tall, ancient and silent trees. Long shadows fell westward where the slanting light from the reclining sun filtered in and overspread an uneven ground. Countless leaves trampled by feet made a crackly noise. The wind rustled as it buffeted against clusters of foliage on tree tops. Birds chirped, perched on a single tree at the opposite end. Other winged species flitted restlessly about the place. The entire forest was an abode of peace. Gazing at the scene, Banarasilal fancied that at any moment a hermit's daughter would emerge from the shades of the forest deep. She would appear freshly bathed, balancing a water vessel on her waist. And he began to dream about a sylvan goddess beckoning him in a soft voice to enter an orchid bower.

But those flights of fancy were brief and anomalous in a land infested with deadly snakes and ferocious animals. Banarasilal and Chandrakanta moved quickly and carefully out of the place. A faint sound of music penetrated their ears as they arrived on the bend. They sensed a great activity somewhere near them, waiting to be discovered. Perhaps, a hermit's but lay hidden behind the woods, after all! And indeed they came upon a wondrous landscape with trees growing on the lean terrain of a distant upland where a corner of the earth had caved in as it was in ancient times. They saw different layers of earth under the transparent water of a stream, flowing like liquefied silver, with a thick stratum of black coal tucked in its midst. Here—many years ago an exhausted fortune hunter had come and made the unexpected discovery of a veritable treasure trove inside the bowels of the earth. To his tired eyes and dejected spirit coming upon that mass of matter must have been the source of unforeseen pleasure.

Water bubbles floated in the air at the hub of the waterfall. Water fell at great speed and flowed encircling islands of stone. The depths of the cascading water and the crystalline stream were visible to the last. Sprays of foam appeared only at places where the current dashed against the boulders. Water flowed over beds of sandy rocks, which had worn away due to the velocity of the current down the ages. All kinds of patterns emerged under the river bed, creating a semblance of a little canyon in that very place. The river journeyed through the deep. Banarasilal had never visited the Grand Canyon nor had he seen the submerged movements of the river Colorado. Now, watching the phenomenon he perceived what it could be like.

They came out and sat on the river bank. Banarasilal began a song without the tanpura at Chandrakanta's request. He went on singing with moist eyes while Chandrakanta listened without stirring. The singing ended at some indefinite moment and the atmosphere becomes one of stunned silence. The sun had gone down behind the range of hills and they felt as if some unspoken secret of life was astir in the woodlands, and in the caverns of the mountains, under the soft moonlight late evening. After sometime Banarasilal stirred and sat up straight. Chandrakanta cleared his throat.

"You have asked me why I was saving money, didn't you?" he asked. Banarasi replied, "Yes."

Chandrakanta moved near and exclaimed, excited, "You are so knowledgeable—you read so many books! Tell me is it possible to bring a dead person back to life?"

Banarasilal was stunned. "Why do you ask?" he said.

"Just like that ..." Chandrakanta became very quiet. After a moment's silence the conversation was resumed.

"I must tell you what I think," he said, "I know how to make a dead man come back to life. I had met a holy man at Secunderbad; he had brought a dead man back to life in front of my eyes. I wouldn't have believed it had I not seen it happen. The man had died because he had touched a coil which a storm had ripped off the power station. He evinced all signs of death by electrocution. The holy man appeared from nowhere, brought out all kinds of things from his *jhola,* and poured them into the mouth of the dead man. He also rubbed all kinds of stuff over his body, singing in a low voice. I had tried to catch the words of his song, but couldn't make head or tail of them. After sometime the stricken man regained consciousness.

Chandrakanta produced a paper from his pocket and began to turn it around. Banarasilal became very curious. "And then ..." he asked.

"The holy man disappeared among the crowd as soon as the man had come round. I had already latched on to him; I followed him all over the place. Finally I was able to pin him down under a tree and shoot all kinds of questions. The holy man kept on laughing, making me more resolute. After much entreaty he agreed to make me his disciple; he was, by then, willing to reveal the secret of his medicine to me. I gave up the construction company job and accompanied him everywhere. I went about the whole of this country. Then one night, on the roadside of Bilaspur town, he handed me this bit of paper with the names of the medicines scribbled on it. Till this day I don't know what made him do that. Besides the names, the exact dosage of the medicines was also inscribed. The medicine has to be administered while singing. The tune of the song sounds curiously like the *Raga Ahir Bhairab*. Ah! yes, it was he who initiated me into the world of classical music. He was an incomparable musician; he sang with such compassion! The medicine is prepared according to a prescription and has to be applied making the sound, "*O Iti Brahma, iti Brahma, iti Brahma*. The holy man left the very next day for some unknown destination. Tell me, what does western science hold out in this regard? Do the dead come back to life?"

Banarasilal found himself in a fix. "Yes," he said. "The murderers are put to sleep on the electric chair in America. Some scientists claim that the tissues of the body remain alive for five to seven minutes after the convicted men are pronounced dead. Attempts are made to resuscitate them if they are still found breathing. Of course, I have only read about it in the newspapers ... I have ..." Chandrakanta became very enthusiastic. "So the people in the west think in the same way too ... but only five to seven minutes? Isn't it possible to make the dead man come alive after a considerably longer time?"

Banarasilal didn't respond to that; Chandrakanta's joy exceeded all bounds.

"I know this to be true," he exulted. "I was singing the same song while I was tying bandages around Matadin's arms. I'm sure I can bring him back to life. The look in his face told me my song had slowed down the effect of poison on his system. But I don't possess the medicines. When the holy man left I realised I had no money and I badly need it to procure medicines, which are all too rare. The medicine consists of a genuine *shilajit* stone which can only be found in secluded mountainous regions, and an oil which is extracted from a flowery shrub that grows exclusively in the valley adjacent to the Manas Sarobar. These medicines are not available in shops, there are others ... I need money to get them. I don't know how long I'll have to stay in the midst of this wilderness to procure the medicines. I plan to set out on my search for the medicines as soon as I have saved up enough money ... do you think rupees five hundred will do?"

Banarsilal had by this time caught the fever! He was as enthusiastic as Chandrakanta. "What rubbish, how can five hundred do? You must have enough to last out one year before you can even start looking for the medicines. Who knows how long it will take you to find them? You'll need five or six thousand rupees at the least to cover the expenses of your journey." Banarasilal said.

Chandrakanta was crestfallen. "Five thousand!" he gasped. "I'll never save up that much even if I were to work all my life! Tell me how does one feel to know that the 'elixir of life' is within your grasp, that you have but to reach out your hand for it and then to discover the innumerable hurdles in the way. I wanted to distribute the medicine among all the people and save so many lives."

Chandrakanta was raving—he wouldn't calm down. His eyes looked frightening. He broke out into laughter, as unexpectedly as he had worked himself up. Finally he gave a loud, resounding laugh for having, at last, found a way out of his dilemma. He threw the crumpled bit of paper into the swirling waters of the mountain stream and stood up. "Let's go," he said. Banarasilal was ready to leave—he cast one last glance at him. Chandrakanta started walking at a furious pace; returning home Banarasilal had difficulty in catching up with him.

The next morning, sipping his morning tea, Banarasilal ruminated about the events of the past evening. The normal, everyday ambience of his surroundings made him feel that the evening's happenings were neither incredible nor a joke. On the contrary, everything that had taken place after Matadin had got bitten by the snake and his arrival at the wondrous mountain site seemed to him as normal as events one gossiped about routinely every day. And sitting beside the worldly-wise Chief engineer, in the clear light of day, he felt sure the poor man had been tricked and had behaved rather foolishly. There was no sense at all in Chandrakanta's throwing away his hard-earned money in this fashion. But Banarasilal wanted to peruse the paper to find out for himself what rubbish the holy man had scribbled on it.

Just then a huge commotion broke out outside the building; excited voices were heard, and the Chief engineer went out to see what the matter was. Looking out of the window, Banarasilal caught the engineer listening intently to a person, who looked like a guard, gesturing and talking animatedly. The engineer returned to the room and collected his jacket and hat. Regarding Banarasilal he said, "Have you any idea, Ostadji, what your dear Chandrakanta has gone and done?"

"What has he done?"

"Last night, at ten-thirty, the assistant manager of the mines was carrying fifteen thousand rupees he had collected at Manendragarh to pay weekly wages to the labourers, fixed for today. He always brought the same amount of money every Friday of the week. That scoundrel Chandrakanta jumped on him from a low branch of a tree midway and completely overpowered him. It was only by chance the car escaped getting bashed up. The assistant manager was armed with a gun, but he couldn't do a thing! I had told him so many times to take a police escort but he wouldn't listen. See now what he has had to suffer for his obduracy! He was beaten senseless and found in that state at six this morning. Fifteen thousand rupees! It's not a joke! The police have gone after the culprit but there's little hope they'll manage to nab him. The man is so cunning ... it won't be easy to apprehend him. What a terrible thing to have happened!"

The engineer left the room in a dazed state, the day passed amidst much turmoil. Chandrakanta was nowhere to be found. Banarasilal decided to return the very same day. He didn't feel like staying on.

So many years have passed since that time, Banarasilal hadn't heard Chandrakanta's name mentioned by anyone again. Nevertheless, he kept on wondering where and how he was.

Perhaps he lay dead in some high mountainous region, or perhaps he was continuing his search on the lonely banks of the lake next to the frosty, intractable Himalayan heights. Banarasilal secretly hoped that the latter were true and that Chandrakanta would return having secured the 'elixir of life.'

There was a particular reason why Banarasilal remembered him after a gap of so many years. He had come across the Chief engineer on the street and hadn't recognized him. He only responded when the engineer called out to him. After conversing about this and that, the engineer mentioned Chandrakanta. Banarasilal couldn't suppress his excitement. He listened without interrupting.

The engineer said:

"Chandrakanta was arrested the very next day. He was found loitering in the vicinity of the waterfall; he had all the stolen money with him. He was muttering to himself, 'I'm looking for the paper everywhere ... where has it gone? Didn't I throw it here.? It had the measures—the dosage of the medicine ... I must find it.' His eyes were blood-shot, his clothes in tatters, his mental condition was utterly chaotic; not a word he said made sense!"

1948

The Earthly Paradise Remains Unshaken

Bhuswarga Achanchal

'It is bitterly cold today'—it's strange how Maqbul Sherwani can think of that one thing over and over again, as he looks steadily at the scarcely visible snow peaks looming in the distance—past the crammed main thoroughfare of Baramulla, past the washed out signboard hung on the second storey of the building standing nearby, and the army of marauders running amuck on the streets. He appears somewhat overwhelmed.

Snow had fallen on the road in Baramulla the night before. It has melted and has become muddy, trampled underfoot by the heavy-booted Afridis and the Momens, wearing thick overcoats with upturned collars. Sherwani reluctantly turns his gaze on them, losing the sight of the mountains. The raiders talk among themselves; they speak the language of the Pakhtoons. Their stubbly faces give off steam in the cold. Looking at them, Sherwani feels much compassion—as if they are not human beings at all, but specimen of the first phase of human evolution—Javaman or Paleolithic beings. Some of them are pulling hard at their cigarettes standing on the opposite side of the street, with their rifles flung on their shoulders. He can see a plinth and a wall among the debris of a bombed-out building; pieces of wood, big and small, lie scattered here and there. A group of famished men, clad in torn kashmiri salwars and wrapped up in thick shawls, have flocked the place like a pack of dogs. Maqbul Sherwani watches everything, bound up with ropes at the top of the staircase of a looted sweet shop.

Ahmadjan sits next to him. Ahmadjan has spent his days fishing in the serene, unruffled waters of the Dal lake, fringed by mountains on its four sides. He has sewed up fish with long, sharp pikes on misty mornings. Now, travelling to the end of the valley, he has come here responding to the call given by the National Conference. He is a small and skinny man, shy and rather timid. His job is to keep sitting in the guerilla camps. They were caught late last night, when the raiders, crossing the hillock, appeared out of the blue in front of them. Sherwani trembles slightly, his head dug in his knees; the thick blanket is hardly adequate to keep off the chill. He has heard stories about women being raped, has seen a woman being tortured, but he was violently shaken by an incident that took place at the crack of dawn, when he was on his way to this place. He came across a girl lying in a ditch a mile up the Baramulla Road. Hearing sounds of several steady feet, the girl was trying to raise herself. She was pregnant. Her torn salwar and kurta were soaked in blood, a blood-stained dopatta rolled in the dust. Who knew how long she had been lying naked in the cold! Her lips were blue. A terrible sight it was! Still conscious the girl had summoned enough strength to come up on the road, but her eyes betrayed fear and anxiety. A few Azad Kashmiri soldiers stood facing her. One of them made a nasty remark, gesturing vulgarly, others laughed. The girl must have died soon after Sherwani left the place.

Azad Kashmiri! So that is the identity of these people! There are some tribals, some British and American among them, as well as Pakistani soldiers, but not a single genuine Kashmiri! The Muslim Conference tried to bring Kashmiris into their fold but few natives of the place had joined them—And is this how they plan to set Kashmir free, make Kashmir an independent country? Maqbul wonders—looting the helpless, raping the women, burning down homes—these people can't be the true followers of Islam. Not they—but the girl who was raped, others like her and the defenceless people who have been thrown out of their houses, whose lands have been robbed by the roaming rogues—they are the real muslims! These men are not human beings at all but beasts or devils. Only money and female bodies seem to rouse them. Sherwani feels simultaneously disgusted and compassionate towards them.

It is October, he knows the bandits have the cards stacked in their favour; he doesn't expect the situation to alter during the winter months. But come spring and the real Kashmiris would be revealed in their true colours; Sher-e-Kashmir will display his might. Sherwani may not live to see that great day—he knows that. They have got him. He is the leader of those who are a nuisance to the bastards! They won't let him off. It is to be expected. He doesn't care. Sherwani is sorry only for Ahmadjan. The poor soul! He has left the relative safety of the banks of the Dal lake and come here. He isn't at all fit for the role he's been given, gets easily worn out; he lacks the agility required of a guerilla fighter. Sherwani gives him a glance. The man is quaking, looking dazed. Is he weeping as well?

Perhaps he is—Sherwani gets irritated. The man would die for sure; he's in for a kick in the pants if he falls at their feet now and begs for mercy. Sherwani pokes him with his knees. Ahmadjan looks up. There are no tears in his eyes but they are glistening. His chin is trembling, perhaps, because of the cold.

"What's the matter?" Sherwani asks, "Are you cold?"

"Yes ... tell me how long will it take for the government troops to arrive?"

He's frightened, of course!

"It's only the beginning of winter," Sherwani replies. "Besides the raiders have just begun their assault. It's unlikely that they will make the scene before the cold gives out. It will be March or April by the time the government sends its troops out here. We have no hope, Ahmadjan!"

"I wasn't thinking of that ... won't Sher-e-Kashmir come here? Won't these people be driven out?" All of a sudden Ahmadjan bends forward.

Maqbul Sherwani firmly replies, "Of course he'll come here. We'll rescue Kashmir from the clutches of these barabarians—even one true Kashmiri alive will make all the difference."

His answer satisfies Ahmadjan. Ahmadjan remains sitting with his face stuck inside the folds of his knees. Lord knows what his thoughts are, he asks such odd questions!

Sherwani turns his face towards the raiders. They are hanging about, busy in their own way. An icy cold breeze stirs up making him feel chilly. He sits bundled up.

Some time passes and a uniformed captain of the group appears on the scene. Sherwani had noticed him earlier; he looks crafty and unreliable. The captain talks to the soldiers and they come forward together. Their heavy boots make a strange sound as they bear down on the ice. Maqbul wires himself up to face the ordeal as they come and stand in front of him. Ahmadjan lifts his eyes—he is fazed; he looks vacantly at the soldiers and remains indifferent as they haul him up.

The two men accompanying the captain are the original Afridis— six feet tall, and of massive build. One of them must have had small pox—his face is full of pock marks—his left eye is squashed. The other has bristles on his chin. Stupid pride is written large on their faces. They are like powerful robots, without an iota of intelligence. They career Ahmadjan towards the captain. Sherwani becomes apprehensive. He is sure that Ahmadjan will blow the gaff as soon as he is interrogated—Ahmadjan is such a coward—he has already shrivelled up—He gets up and tries to catch Ahmadjan's attention, but finds a man pointing a rifle at him. The captain who was watching everything comes forward now and the two men drag Ahmadjan to his front. The captain points Sherwani to Ahmadjan. "Is he your leader?" Ahmadjan nods absentmindedly. Sherwani has no doubt that Ahmad is still engrossed in that one thought he has had in his mind since the day before. The captain looks derisively at Maqbul, and turns to Ahmadjan. "What's your name?"

"Ahmadjan,"

"Good, now listen carefully Ahmadjan! We'll let you off. You can go free if you give us the names of the guerillas, show us the camps. Can't you see how well we are paid to do our job? You'll get a fat sum if you act wisely. We need a true Kashmiri patriot like you. The Kashmiris won't remain duped by Hindu India or the Indian government!"

Maqbul looks at Ahmadjan full of fear, but Ahmadjan is lost in thought. He has heard nothing. The captain loses his patience. "Can't you hear," he hollers, "A lot of money is involved. Your life will also be spared ... Has the man gone deaf? Can you hear me? Abdullah's men will be defeated. Make use of the opportunity you have now ...

The mention of Abdullah makes Ahmadjan prick up his ears; words begin to form in his mouth.

"Bastards! The Sheikh will come here for sure." He repeats the words again and again like a wound up doll as he moves close to the captain and spits on his face.

Taken aback, the captain jerks his face away. The two soldiers ready their gun at him but Ahmadjan keeps his ground; he doesn't seem to care. It's the chilly wind that bothers him. The captain, red in the face, takes out a handkerchief. Ahmadjan is now on his feet. He sends forth a volley of abuse.

"Dogs!" he shouts.

The captain takes his pistol out—his hands are shaky. He puts it back into its cover after a thought. He orders the black soldier to take Ahmadjan's shawl away. Unwrapped, Ahmadjan stands with only an ordinary shirt and a vest on. One by one he's stripped of all his clothes until he is left with only a salwar in the cold. To Sherwani's eyes Ahmadjan's body has already become bluish in the chilly wind.

Ahmadjan has not made things difficult for the raiders in any way; he has helped them rather. Now he grits his teeth and throws insults at them, "Dogs! Death to you," he says.

It is too much for the captain. He kicks him hard with his heavy boots and pushes him headlong on to the brittle, shimmering ice. Sherwani shudders but Ahmadjan is as unconcerned as ever. He turns to Sherwani as the one-eyed soldier leaves.

"Didn't I do the right thing?" he asks him.

"You ..." Maqbul begins, but the soldiers have their grip on his wrists and he is unable to say more. The one-eyed soldier brings an unhinged shutter of a broken-down door he finds in the debris. The captain indicates that it be placed on top of Ahmadjan's chest.

Maqbul is restless now, "Scum of the earth," he mutters to himself. Aloud he says, "I'm sure you..." The captain who has turned around on his heels looks at him mockingly. "Shut up!" he shouts.

Maqbul shuts his eyes. The soldiers have climbed up the wooden frame and are pressing it down Ahmadjan's body with their feet. Ahmadjan doesn't cry out, he doesn't groan, he merely gulps and repeats, "Dogs!" with great difficulty.

Thick, blackish-red blood begins to ooze from his nose, his mouth. He dies within minutes.

The soldiers rejoice at their feat and kick the wooden door away. The captain is hardly bothered. He turns his attention to Maqbul.

"So ... you are the leader? Well, well!"

A man from among the assembled Kashmiris comes out now. His face is familiar to Maqbul—an inhabitant of the place? Maybe. He whispers something into the captain's ears, and at once the captain raises his brows. "Is that so?" The Kashmiri gives an ugly laugh. "I'll remember what you've said," the captain adds. Turning to Maqbul he addresses him, "Maqbul Sherwani Sahab, Adabaraz! A leader of the National Conference, no less! My greetings to you!" The captain lights up a cigarette and salutes Sherwani tauntingly.

"So ... it's you who created all the rumpus when Quaid-i-Azam came to Baramulla to rest?"

Sherwani smiles sweetly. "Not at all ... I just went up on the platform where Mr Jinnah was sitting and said a few words to him, that's all. In Srinagar, Mr Jinnah had declared to the Sheikh Saheb he wouldn't meddle in our internal affairs, yet soon afterwards, as a representative of the Muslim Conference, he started to make contrary noises in different gatherings. He was doing the same thing here—spreading communalism. That's why I had to go and tell him a few things. He became so frightened that he fled the place with the help of some Dogra soldiers. Do you know those you consider wicked and mischief mongers regard Baramulla as the heart and soul of India. Mr Jinnah had to run away from this place with life in his hands!" The captain's face becomes crimson. Furious he leaves at once, mumbling a faint "Yes.".

Maqbul turns his thoughts to Ahmadjan who he had considered a weakling. Ahmadjan was incapable of joining words together; he was always longing to get back to the Dal lake, almost from the moment he had arrived. How did the same person become so strong all of a sudden?

The captain preoccupies himself kicking pieces of wood lying scattered on the ground. He carries on a desultory conversation with his men. At times he points to the bombed-out building. Sherwani sits down when he quits the place.

Some time passes. Sherwani observes the soldiers are removing the wreckage and building a cross, joining together small and big pieces of wood. The cross is then dug deep into the rubble.

The captain returns to the scene wiping his mouth, after a meal perhaps. Maqbul is led to the broken down building. He stops stunned besides Ahmadjan's corpse. The soldiers keep mum. Sherwani gazes at the drawn face of Ahmadjan; blood streaming out of his nostrils has collected into a pool. He gives him a salute.

"Salam, Ahmadjan! The associate of Sher-e-Kashmir, Maqbul Sherwani salutes you! Sheikh Abdullah salutes you! All of Kashmir salutes you! A day will come when the whole of India will salute you. Today you lie abandoned on the Baramulla highway, in front of the marauders, but you are a symbol of a strong and silent resistance. Khuda Hafez!"

The snow-clad peaks jut out from the far reaches of the valley. The wrinkles on the body of the mountains are enveloped in mist. Their contours have become hazy suggesting a deep mystery. The chilly wind builds into a minor storm. Flakes of ice escaping the crevices on the street flutter in the air. Objects near at hand become a blur. The sun, having already hidden itself behind a thin veil of cloud, after a fleeting appearance, spreads its dim brilliance all over the place. Maqbul Sherwani walks ahead.

It is a replay of a two thousand year old history; a spiritless rerun of a momentous event. Maqbul is actually tied up on the cross which is dug deep in the smoothed out remains of the plinth of the bombed building. A soldier arrives with large nails and a hammer. The captain contemplates the scene with amusement. The Kashmiri folk crowd in like a kennel of dogs; the leader of the National Conference is put to the proof. His interrogation begins.

"Look Sherwani," the captain moves closer, "I'm sure you're not as stupid as the man over there ... You know what is good and what is bad for you. I don't want to kill you, I'll be sorry if I have to. The brave respects the brave. Listen, I won't kill you if you are not hostile to us. You won't suffer, I assure you. So many men of the National Conference have come over to our side. We can offer you a good civilian position, but you know well what the consequences are if you don't comply with our wishes. But I believe you see my point."

Sherwani doesn't utter a word. He knows about the men who have gone over to the enemy camp: the cowards and the greedy. He also knows what lies behind the captain's offer. His betrayal would provide grist to the rumour mill and fill the newspaper columns. There is no doubt in his mind that his double cross is more important to these men than the independence of Kashmir.

The captain shouts, "Long lives Azad Kashmir!" The soldiers take up the slogan which rents the air. The captain wonders whether he should spit on Sherwani's face—No, that would be too barbaric—he decides.

"Death to Azad Kashmir!" Sherwani's voice is clear and loud. He stresses every word he utters.

The captain narrows his eyes and laughs; he flings a taunt.

"Showing off your might for a dare, are you?" He orders the soldiers to nail Sherwani up.

The blind man hammers the nail into Maqbul's left hand, stretched out on a wooden plank. Maqbul clenches his teeth and shuts his eyes. The captain laughs, "I see, your courage is deserting you already!" No, he must not weaken—Maqbul thinks—the beasts, they do not know that Kashmiris don't totter under extreme oppression. "You think that because you are here, the entire people of this country will become traitors? Long live Sher-e-Kashmir, long live the Government of Kashmir!" He shouts.

The captain's exasperation knows no bounds. He taps the ground with his feet. "No more delay," he shouts to his men.

And thereafter begins another glorious chapter in the history of Modern India. With one blow of the hammer, the sharp end of the nail goes through Sherwani's soft palms and pierces the wood. Blood trickles from his fingers. Sherwani feels as if a hurricane of flame is ignited inside his entrails with each and every blow. He feels sparks of fire all over his body and he writhes in pain as the soldiers inflict deep gashes on his feet and hands. Maqbul grits his teeth. The captain jeers at him "Will you still give the National Conference call?" he asks. Sherwani's silence infuriates him. "Nail him up on the right hand," he orders the soldiers.

The pain is excruciating! Maqbul feels he has reached the limits of his endurance. But he doesn't give in and shouts, "Long lives the Kashmir Government!" The captain is beside himself hearing him shout. He kicks Maqbul, bestowing hard blows on his eyes, his face, oblivious of the world. There are deep wounds on Maqbul's cheeks, blood comes out of his mouth; it tastes salty. The mob moves back. The sight has been too much for them.

Sherwani's head swims; his forehead has a huge bump but he opens his blood-shot eyes and shouts again, "Long live Sher-e-Kashmir." The words whack the brain of the captain like a hammer stroke. He screams like a mad dog. "Finish him off; I order you, don't delay!" The one-eyed soldier dithers. Does the robot too have a soul?

"He's dead," he tells the captain. Another round of blows and Maqbul's head doesn't feel achy anymore; his sinews have stopped functioning; he's not one jot sensible of anything. He still stares at the captain, and with an utmost effort of will shouts, "Death to Azad Kashmir!"

Maqbul's body is riven with so many nails, yet the distant snowy peaks are baring their glory. The valley appears breathlessly picturesque. The sky that had turned grey is slowly fading out of sight. It's wonderful—this paradise on earth! The tree in Maqbul's family house is covered with snow now. He has etched so many strange patterns on the virgin ice collected on its cornices and on its tin roof.

One day the tree will again luxuriate in the colour green, get covered with tender leaves and flowers. The valley will become alive. The vineyards would bend under the weight of juicy grapes and a coverlet of young grass spread over the entire valley like a soft kashmiri shawl. Spring cannot be far behind if winter is already here!

The soldiers would march in with the coming of Spring. They would arrive in hordes, tracking the precarious heights, crossing the dangerous ravines, building bridges over the rivers, led in the front, by a tall and huge hulk of a man. He will take big strides and come here—the Lion of Kashmir! These dogs will disappear, flee at his sight.

Kashmir will be built anew, the Kashmir of Maqbul's dreams, whose people don't grovel at the feet of the Dogra kings—but Kashmir for the Kashmiris, the earthly paradise!

The captain tells his men, "Bring the body down ... he's dead." Maqbul's dizziness clears for a second as the words travel to his ears, faint as if they are coming from a long distance.

"Sheikh Abdullah zindabad!" he repeats. But the captain now exhausted, goes down the stairs, dispirited, and walks away. He lights a cigarette and orders his men to stand in a file and hold up their rifles. A havildar stands by to direct the operation.

To Maqbul Sherwani all of it is a smudged canvas. The earth seems to have crumpled up and become very small. Images of his past life float in his mind's eyes like in the movies: the entire trajectory of his life's experience. He is not sorry about anything. His life is pure like the barely visible mountain spire. He has no regrets—he has given his whole life to the cause. Death seems to have come to him as a fitting end.

He had done what was good for the country —is still doing what is best for it. One day the Kashmiris will adopt his path ...

He dies after a thirteen round of bullets.

1948

The Crystal Goblet

Sfatikpatra

The famed dust of Delhi streets, about which songs were sung, and which, as the saying goes, had at one time driven, the Moghuls and the Sikhs alike, into a frenzy—no longer floats in the air.

It's pointless to look for it—it simply doesn't exist. There's no danger, therefore, of children of nice gentlemen falling ill, infected by the invisible germs borne by it. The wide Delhi highways are now obscured by a different breed—bands of displaced, homeless refugees.

At least that's the impression I had when I got off the mail train the other day. There wasn't standing space in the platform, in the shed, or anywhere else for that matter. The entire place was packed with human beings enacting the great drama of life: giving birth to babes or dying of old age—the perennial stage show of the mortals! The flimsy veil of decency that covered this drama was now being ripped apart by a barbaric insolence.

I was much amused by the sight. These people, who had been living happily unperturbed in Lahore, Layalpur, Muzaffarbad or Multan till only the other day, have been thrown back now to life's primordial conditions, shorn of all semblances of civilization—due to a sudden change in their circumstances. It was amazing!

I am a government servant—another officer of the state is my relative. He also happens to be my boss and the intermediary between myself and the government at the Center. It's no use making a secret of it; I was able to secure this job without any effort due to his good offices. I am here to butter him up, and the occasion—his son's *annaprasan* (rice eating) ceremony. This was the first time my wretched self has set his foot in Delhi, the jewel of India 's crown, and I must confess I was a bit shaken by this kind of welcome to the ancient, populous city. Deep in my heart I had hoped that I would get some feel of the splendour that was once medieval India. My misfortune was that I lived in a vulgar age when it was foolish to have such dreams!

Away from it all ... I managed to arrive at New Delhi's Nasratbag district sitting on a carriage called the 'tonga' which carried me half aloft the air and half scraping against the ground. Nasratbag, according to the pack of imbeciles, the bureaucrats, the greatest gift of the British empire to India, was an aristocratic neighbourhood. My relative, a high ranking officer, was an honourable member of the locality. I don't want to burden my memory by recalling the details of the elaborate celebrations that were drawn up for the festive occasion. I was already very curious about the homeless people I had seen on the road. I am told that it was unseemly curiosity that was the death of the great discoverers and hunters of old. Alas! I too, led on by curiosity, got involved in a dangerous business. Let me tell you how...

I sauntered along a road to the refugee camp, at some distance from Delhi, to have a look at this new tribe of beggars. I'll never in my life forget the scene I saw: a refugee slum newly erected out of dried-up stalks of crops in the middle of a field. I moved from place to place only to discover it was the same scene everywhere. I was reminded of the bare necessities of life simply because those appeared non-existent. Filthy, tattered clothes and despairing looks made up a stark picture of naked pauperism. How the meager straw thatching could ward off the sharp sting of the January cold was certainly something one could make the subject of research!

A cholera epidemic was rampant among them at that time. A group of nurses had arrived to look after the patients. I saw a girl being inoculated in a room. A lot of hairs hung loosely about her face, smeared with vomit, flies were swarming around her. As I came to the veranda and pressed a handkerchief against my nose wondering whether the place was not some kind of hell, real or mythical, I was taken back by the sound of a heart-rending wail. It had risen from a room at the opposite end, and was gradually melting into a stifling sob. I went forward to see what more revelations were in store for me.

There was a mother and a child—the perennial subject of the Madonna pictures! The girl must have been pretty sometime in the remote past; now she looked unclean and had a pained and panic-stricken expression on her face. She was groaning and saying something. I could catch only some of her slurred words—"Mera munna, mera lal." She was sitting with her feet apart and pulling at her hair; her mouth was dripping with saliva. A beautiful child, gasping and on the point of death lay in front of her. The sound of her cry had brought others, besides me, running to the place. One of them sent for the doctor. He arrived with a crowd of curious bystanders following him from behind. The doctor sat beside the child, took his pulse and shook his head. Raising my head from one corner of the crowded room, I saw the mother, seeing so many people, give a start, quickly pick up the pile of blanket the child had kicked away, and retire into a corner, staring wildly around her. She started to move among the people as soon as the crowd began to thin and came outside. Breaking the silence of the room, the doctor spoke out in a resounding voice, "It's all over, orderly." I was regarding the mother. She had gone still—her fists were clenched—she was taking a deep breath. She went out to the veranda at the back, staring at me for a while. The doctor enquired whose child it was. Someone replied, "She was here a minute ago... I can't see her now."

I was curious to find out more about the rare phenomenon; I followed the woman and came outside. She was sitting in one corner of the veranda wrapping herself up nicely with the blanket. As I drew near her I saw the dense expression on her face, as if all her emotions were packed, frozen there. But her lips were still quivering, and she was humming the world's oldest lullaby, "Munna mera, mere lal... lal mera..."

"Maiji, why did you go out. They are looking for you all over the place..." I said. The girl laughed in a silly manner, changing her position. Then she made an inaudible sound and went silent.

"They're going to take the child away, dear... speak to them or something strange and unthinkable will be done..." I said emphasising.

"Strange and unthinkable!" the girl repeated. I noticed she spoke *hindusthani* with a slant stressing the consonants rather heavily. She regarded me for some time, then gazed outside; her lips were moving and she continued to whine. After sometime she wiped her dripping nose with her dirty dopatta and resumed her silence. What was she looking out at—I wondered. There were the resplendent sun and the lustrous green fields—the life-giving radiance that sustained this earth. Who had told her she had the right to look at them?

Two persons emerged carrying the child in a string cot. She was startled by the sound of their footsteps, and looked up apprehensively. I kept looking at how a curl of her coarse, blonde hair kept billowing in the wind as she vigorously shook her head. Her lips were slightly apart as if she wanted to cry her heart out. But she stifled her sobs by pressing her mouth with her two dirty, petal-like hands.

People carrying the dead child left the place. Overcome with pity, I tried to say something, fingering the corner of her blanket. I didn't know what I could say—my views had always remained unspoken—like a flash the girl jerked away before I could open my mouth.

"Don't, don't ... take that—I feel cold." She exclaimed and resumed moaning.

"Don't be afraid, I'm not one of them," I said. "Why do you behave like that?"

The girl spoke out harshly now. "They'll take it away if they come to know who the blanket belongs to... in these terribly cold days." She began to weep again, murmuring in a trembling voice, "Munna mera, lal mere."

At last I comprehended the situation. The girl had left the land of the five rivers and had come to this place to build a home in these parts. She had arrived with a child and a modicum of decency. The blanket was all she possessed. The child must have used it to protect itself from the cold even the night before. People would have simply thrown it away as a germ-ridden rug had she introduced herself to them. She must have witnessed that happen to others; the experience had provided her with this strange way to express her motherly feelings! Those who are interested in taking, merely take without wanting to give anything back in return.

Newly enlightened I regarded the girl once more. She was still gazing at the scene outside, reclining her head in a familiar manner. I felt as if I was beholding the primitive earth from the planet Mars, at a time when the earth's history consisted of its watery phenomenon. The endless rain, howling winds, and permanently overcast horizon must have made melancholy music, and the perpetual downpour must have sent off sounds of despair. I wondered how much of all the moaning noise could have reached Mars!

No doubt what I then felt was a pure upsurge of emotions—I am helpless; I am not capable of surrendering my own comforts in succour of others. It's the plain truth. So many people witness such scenes, and buy cinema tickets the next minute. I'm no better.

The experience should have cured me completely of the desire to have more of the same—I was sure I would be stifled to death if I remained in the obnoxious atmosphere a minute longer. It was unmannish sentimentality that must have had made me touch the body of that abandoned woman. Lord save me... I rushed out of the place, sure I would die of cholera if by chance I had caught the infection. I ran with the speed of a meteor flying through the sky, holding the handkerchief to my nose, while I glanced back at the world I was deserting. The pose I struck reminded me of the one Chakrabarti Rajagopalchari assumed when he went on an inspection tour of the Calcutta slums, and pictures were taken to fill up the last pages of the *Statesman*.

Fate was against me—my temperament only added to my predicament. I had always been inquisitive, especially when it came to observing the animal kind. I can't remember at which point I wanted to turn away from the naked truth ... but like Yuddhistir of yore I wasn't inclined to conclude observing the world.[1]

Coming out of the hutments I noticed that a new band of refugees, traversing vast distances, had descended there. The sight was something! Like an idiot I tarried to have a look. Do you think I would have stayed back had I any inkling of the troubles I would be beset by? The provocation came in the shape of an old man. From his dust-covered headgear to the nagra on his feet, that ancient soul was the embodiment of an elegy. In any case, I had already decided he couldn't be spreading the cholera germ! Every fold in his face, every pore of his skin contributed to make him the living image of the authentic Indian, such as one sees in colourful English magazines. The veins on his hands

1. Yuddhistir, the eldest of the five Pandava brothers, is depicted in the *Mahabharata* as a man 'capable of self-deception like most men', and with a prosperity to be 'caught in peripheral involvements, transient gratifications.'

stood out prominently; he wore a pathetic look. I was sure his life couldn't have been all poetry—a thing of Beauty! Seeing that I looked spick and span, he came straight to me—couldn't he have left me alone? What can I say... the fellow simply destroyed my peace of mind!

Clutching a piece of paper in his fist he asked, "Are you a Hindu?" I nodded. He thought for a while, and said, "Dear Hindu brother, can you give me information about an address?" He looked conspiratorial, my wretched curiosity rose leaps and bounds. "What's the address?" I asked.

The man looked furtively here and there and coming forward brought his smelly face next to mine, "Do you know the address of the government?"—I had wished to God he hadn't come so close, the smell sickened me—

"Government... what government?" I asked.

The man was visibly annoyed, "Oh dear! I mean the government of this country, the government of India. I have to see him rather urgently!"

"*See him?*" I repeated incredulous. "You old ass, the government is not a person ... there are so many people, you and I, all of us! We all make up the government."

I wondered whether I should enlighten him about the composition of our national parliament and our Constitution Bill, but concluded that it would be too much for his old brain to take in. So I ended with a flourish, and declared our glorious ideal: "The State consists of all of us, me, you and others—"

Now it was his turn to get baffled. He gulped. "You mean to say, the state, the government is not a person? What am I to do then? Who ought I to see?"

He looked totally lost at not being able to keep his special tryst with the great nation-state. I felt pity for him.

"Okay then—if see you must—why not look up Pandit Jawaharlal Nehru—he is the head of the State after all."

"Panditji, Panditji ..." the man repeated the name and seized my hand. "Write down his name, please ... I won't remember it." He must have thought I was someone he could jabber away with. I carefully removed my hand, wiped it clean with my handkerchief. I said, irritated, "You haven't heard of Panditji? The whole world knows about him. Where do you come from, pray?"

The man looked small and withdrew into himself. I knew the symptom only too well. I had seen children become quiet with shame when we scolded them in the midst of our showering them with affection; the tone the peasants adopted when they spoke to those they were reprimanded by, those they assumed were sympathetic to their cause and to whom they expressed their sorrows. The old man now assumed the tone of a slave addressing his master.

"I belong to Layalpur ... I worked as day labourer in the fields."

I felt sorry for him all over again. "Old man, what business do you have with Panditji?" I asked trying to be warm towards him. He opened out quite dramatically, as if he wanted to tell me everything.

"Babuji, I have a petition. This is the list of my belongings." The man released a paper from his fist and let me into his big secret: a cot, two buffaloes, one plough, clothes, other movables! I was suitably impressed. I returned the paper and asked, "What's all this for?"

"To show it to Government so that *he* gives me back my things." He sounded so positive.

My head was reeling; I wanted to double up with laughter.

"You have left them all behind; do you think that if you ask Panditji you—"

"That's what they've told me...they said I would get everything back in the land of my Hindu brothers." He was clear enough!

I was beginning to feel a real compassion for him but decided I wouldn't utter a word. The man must be off his head!

"Won't Panditji give me back my belongings even if I were to make a request?" He repeated his question. What could I do but smile and say a muted yes. He looked up thinking of something. His companions had spread their tattered rugs and were talking among themselves. I wondered what they had to say to each other.

"Babuji, where does Panditji live?" he asked.

"In Delhi."

"Delhi!" The man was simply delighted. "Delhi is close by, is it not?'

I couldn't tell him that Delhi was a long way from the place; there were 'miles to go'.

The man sank into a deep silence. I decided not to harass the old codger by giving him false hopes. I cleared my throat, "Look, I don't know who has put those ideas into your head. Whoever he maybe, he has given you false comfort and done you a great disservice. You'll never get anything back. Give up the hope... and there's not much point in seeking a meeting with Panditji; he's difficult to come by—you may never get to see him..."

I had progressed thus far in my speech, looking the other way and waving my hands when I suddenly caught the expression on his face. He was listening to every word I had uttered without slightly moving his face muscle. The paper was still in his fist. His muscle bound hand which had held the plough and had tilled the land was quaking. It was the hand of India's working class! The next minute the man broke down. He wept and tore the paper into pieces. I was still watching...

After some moments he lifted his eyes and gazed directly at me. My soul trembled! The tears had vanished; instead his eyes were blazing with fury. His intrepid looks and resolute chin bore the signature of the ultimate resolve of a man who had lost everything. He got up and said with a tear-soaked voice, adding an extra emphasis to each word he uttered, "Who's the enemy... the enemy? I'll crack open his skull, finish him off, once I identify him. I'm sure I will... I'll find him out one day and that day ..." the man thunderously concluded: "Yes, I'll live to see that day, without doubt."

Good heavens! Its sedition, I thought, worse than the cholera germ, more dangerous! I ran out of the place into the main road. It was a terrible experience!

It is evening now. I have thought of the man all day long. I have come here as a guest to attend the festivities which are *de riguer* for an occasion like the *annaprasan*. But those words keep flitting across my mind: 'Munna mera, Lal mera and 'Delhi is close by,' and 'I'll crack open the skull...' I look at other guests unknowingly as I raise my hand to my throat. My host startles me by his sudden appearance. He beckons me to follow him and sit among those who are my friends. I lift a glass of wine.

"Munna mere, Lal mere..." such a monotonous whine! Layalpur! Where's Layalpur? Is wheat cultivated there? And the enemy, who is the enemy? I take a deep breath, finish the drink in one gulp, then sit balancing the goblet in the air. There is froth on its walls, irradiating in the illumination. I am in its midst.

I gaze at my reflection in the crystal goblet. What else can I do?

1949

Eyes

Chokh

Andlay remained standing. "Why do you look startled from time to time, Ray?" Ray cast his big, blood-shot eyes at him, rubbed them, and wiped his face with a handkerchief. "Not really," he protested, giving a smile.

"But you do ... I have been in your room all this time ... you've become so thin in the last few days." Mr. Andlay sat down facing Ray.

Ray continued cracking his slim fingers, wondering whether he ought to tell Andlay about the dream he had had. That was out of the question! Lord knew what Andlay would make of it; besides—he shuddered, pulled his chair and sat up—it must have been a dream! He found Andlay keenly watching him. Does it mean he had been behaving strangely? No, he mustn't give in to such neurotic thoughts! Ray gathered himself and asked, laughing, "What brings you here, Andlay?"

Andlay pressed his elbows against the table, "The tribunal has finally given a verdict in our favour. The boss, I'm sure, has already collected his insurance money ... I know the hard work you've put in at Allahabad. But look at it this way—luck has turned in your favour. The boss is about to sack the old dodderer Nausherbanji and appoint you as the spinning master. What's more ... Ah yes! How much did you collect from our Allahabad head office?" Andlay leaned forward and grinned. The smile on Ray's face faded, giving place to anxiety. Ray was no longer looking at Andlay but at the sunless yard behind, past the side doors. What were they, the two glittering spots in the dark? Were they eyes? Rukminia's two large, petal-like eyes? Still, calm and indifferent? What were those eyes saying? What does that look mean? Ray felt disturbed.

There was no sound about the place save for the suppressed swishing noise coming from the blow-room and the wagons clashing infrequently in the distant shunting yard.

Andlay looked at Ray amazed. Ray's lips were quivering ... what was there in the empty yard at his rear that could have roused Ray's interest. He was behaving in such an odd manner, giving a start every now and then.

"Are you unwell?" Andlay asked. Ray winced, "Not at all ... I mean, I'm ok."

"What's the matter then? Really, you shouldn't have come to work the moment you got off the train ... You've been under a great strain. Doesn't matter, relax. I'm going around the time office. See you tomorrow evening. I'll come to your bungalow!" Andlay got up.

Ray shook his head in a slow motion; he could barely take in what Andlay said. Advancing towards the blow-room, Andlay paused and with his hands on the swing-door looked back at Ray.

Ray tried hard to act normal. "What's the matter now?" he asked. Making frequent pauses, Andlay began, "that's what I had come to tell you ... I mean, the attendance today is one fourth the normal. Only those who are loyal have turned up.

"Why?"

"A lot has taken place while you were away. Someone has drilled into them that the warehouse was deliberately set on fire to claim insurance money and destroy the contraband goods, and all such nonsense—they think that the murder—" Ray jumped to his feet, abandoning his seat; he looked distressed. Andlay frowned. Ray forced a smile.

"Tell me what happened next."

"They say you had a hand in the murder—they are spreading all kinds of rumours. They held a meeting this afternoon—after they got to know about the verdict. They are demanding an independent enquiry—and they've threatened not to join work."

Ray was standing, gripping the corner of the table with his hands; his finger knuckles appeared white under the glare of the lamp.

"That son of Rukminia is really strange," Andlay said. "Doesn't he work at the doubling? He's called Andu or some other ... Well, he's turned up. He's working in the night shift ... Ok, you take rest."

This time, the time office-in-charge, Andlay really left. The swing door came to a stop after oscillating a few times. Ray sat down again. He felt nice running his fingers through his hair and unsettling them. The affair had been pressing him down ever since he got off the train. The events of the past few days had been churning inside his mind. He couldn't rid his thoughts of them. They took on an even more sinister shape in his dreams. It were better he stayed awake and mulled them over, far better! The glass top of the table was cracked. Ray went on scratching it with his nails and worrying.

The incident had taken place nine days ago in the commercial hub of Kanpur, on the premises of Ratanlall Cotton Mills, situated in Kalpi Road. Work was on, in full swing, in the night. Ray, a great favourite of Ratanlall Gupta, was in charge of spinning. Some hours were left for the night to end, when he was summoned by the peon to appear at the office of Saxena, the PA to the managing agent. Ray was taken aback! The PA rarely came to the mill at night. Of course, there was some tension among the workers, and the PA was obliged to visit the place, but what was the need to call him up? Ray had left the factory and had gone into the office building full of anxiety.

Ray least wanted to recall what he, sleepy-eyed, had heard the PA tell him that terrible night. There was nothing unusual about what he had said save a proposal. Ray was aware the union was upto all kinds of tricks to enforce a search of the warehouse. They had even informed the police station at one time. The matter had been nipped in the bud after considerable effort. Then the workers had started to keep a day and night watch over every lorry going out of the place. The watch and ward staff had among them men belonging to the union. There was no hope, whatsoever, of transporting anything outside quantities of cotton wool without their coming to know about it. The establishment already had information that the agitation had spread to Allahabad and Lucknow. Ray hadn't worried his head over the matter—it was not his headache. But he had no doubt that this time round the bosses were in for a drubbing. Ray was landed with the PA's proposal in the middle of all this. The warehouse was situated in the yard next to his room. He had to manage the job that very night. He didn't have to exert himself too much; gallons of petrol were kept in cans next to sacks of rice beyond the doors sealed by the Insurance Company. The money involved was large enough to make him gasp. He knew that his career advancement would be a smooth affair once he was able to please the bosses. Ray had nerves of steel, fit to accomplish the impossible. He came out of the PA's room ready for the job. Nevertheless, he stopped twice, on his way out of the office premises, and pondered over the matter. The porter of the inner gate saluted him as he let him in. Entering the place Ray hesitated, thinking he should have discussed the matter through with the PA. The warden closed the door and looked up at Ray with surprise. The man was known to Ray—the fellow was one of that union men. Ray straightened up and strode inside the Blow-room.

Bales of pressed cotton were released from the sacks, loosened and then thrown inside the one-story high funnel in the Blow-room. They were beaten, made soft and pushed by air through a long funnel, at the end of which were bowls where the sorted cotton wool came to rest. The workers lifted baskets piled up with cotton and carried them away to the next room for cutting.

It was mostly women who were busy loosening the tightly pressed cotton that night. Factory laws didn't permit women to be employed during night shift, but the situation was special. An order for a large consignment had arrived; the women had been brought in as additional labour force. Rukminia was prominent among them. She was perhaps fifty years old, a strong and youthful looking woman with a head full of white hair. Ray felt an aversion towards her. He regarded her as aggressive and dubious. As for her glance, he couldn't make any sense of it, no matter how hard he tried. His blood boiled at the way she looked at her bosses or her favourites.

She was the ring leader of the union and was given to making inflammatory speeches. A large number of workers were at her beck and call. The labour officer was Ray's source of information. Ray found her sitting and dozing, her hands free of work. He shouted at her using filthy language. Taken aback the woman gave him a reluctant salute and started to work, throwing him wary looks. But her eyes were calm as before. Physically revolted, Ray returned to his office. When he looked back, forcing his way against the swing door of his office, he saw the woman still gazing at him steadfastly, sitting at the opposite end of the illuminated factory shed. She turned her face away as soon as their eyes met.

Ray entered his room knowing fully well the woman was angry with him; he was aware that a strict boss earned the subordinate's wrath. But that didn't mean she had to stare at him in such a baffling manner. He didn't feel like bothering about it; he had a task to accomplish. He felt restless and couldn't sit down. His body was tingling all over and his mind was agitated. There was not much left of the night and hardly any time to lose. Ray took out the tool box from a drawer of his desk and placed it on top of the table. Then for some reason he pushed the swing door wide and had another look at the Blow-room. He found the darwan of the inner gate standing in front of Rukminia—what was he doing there, he wondered; he frowned and called out to him. The darwan came and gave him a salute. Ray interrogated him in a gruff voice. The warden showed him a book and told him that Bankelalbabu, the time keeper, had asked for a doubling supervisor; he had come there to find one. Dismissing him Ray came back to his room. With swift hands, he tied together pieces of gunny cloth lying in one corner, and went out to the yard carrying the tool box and a torch. The yard was completely dark; there was no one in sight. The warehouse was covered in silence. Under the suffused light of the stars against the canvas of the night's sky, the warehouse looked demonic. The agitation within Ray made him feel sick. His heart pounded so furiously he thought its sound could be heard from a great distance. After some moments of stunned stillness, Ray melted away, without a sound, in the darkness on the other side of the wall.

Apart from the familiar voices of the lead workers making a racket in the machine shop at the other end, there was no other noise. What was that fellow saying to Rukminia? Ray had begun to detest the atmosphere inside the factory; it had become so bizarre! He must keep an eye on that woman—sack her at the first opportunity.

The warehouse window was situated high above him; there was a ladder-like iron staircase leading up to the terrace next to it. Ray had to go up the ladder to reach the door sealed by the Insurance Company. Saxena had told him the window could be unfastened from the outside; it was unbarred. Ray knew he could lay the blame on a spark given off by a rotten electric wire.

The iron rungs of the ladder had gone slippery with dew—

Ray could hardly grasp them. He sat on the top of the ladder and gazed down at the dark yard below and the shed at a distance. He began to sort out the instruments of the tool box. He wasn't that easily upset; his bosses thought of him as a man with steely nerves—was that a mistake? Why were his hands trembling? His face lit up with a faint smile. His bosses had supreme faith in him—that's why he had been entrusted with the most difficult job. The window on the top opened out to money, to success and fame! He had no doubt that a few moments effort that night would bring him a lifetime of comfort, security and happiness!

He worked fast. The window flung open making a faint noise. He wiped his hands clean and put the screwdriver back into the box. It was pitch dark inside. He stuck his head in and looked around, lit the torch cautiously and flashed it all over the place. Rows of sacks lay piled, one on top of the other. Getting down wasn't a problem! He went down swiftly and lit the torch once again as he came below stepping over the sacks. Saxena Saheb had indicated that the way to the dump of contraband goods lay in the east. A few petrol cans were kept in front of the entrance to the room. The job was easy enough. He tried to calculate which was the eastern corner. But the atmosphere was beginning to stifle him. It was so stuffy that he found it difficult to breathe. The darkness inside the warehouse made him feel cold and frightened. Scared, he took hasty steps eastward. The wooden lid of the floorboard lay behind rows of sacks. The flash from Ray's torch glanced off the cans of petrol. He lifted up one of them, broke the seal, removed the stopper, and then poured its entire content around the wooden lid. He quickly took another and scattered its content right up to the window. He was getting increasingly restless. He brought another can and emptied it over the sacks. He lost count of the times he repeated the action. He was in a daze, perspiring profusely by the time he had emptied out all the petrol in store and stood resting his hands on his haunch. He felt weak. Wiping his face he moved up, slowly stepping over the sacks till he reached the bottom of the window. Suddenly there was a sound of human breath. Ray felt he would faint. He moved near the window. His heart began to throb. Ray knew the company would come out clean in the whole affair, and it would be he who would have to bear the brunt. He couldn't imagine his fate—a broken man without a future! His eyes stung. Who was that? Motionless, he let his eyes roam over the place.

A faint shadow of a human head wobbled up and went down. Ray waited, feeling quite murderous. The head bobbed up again and pair of eyes peered in; slowly the head hung out as if to take a look at the goings-on in the factory. Rays two hands flew at the throat like a flash—a stifled cry stopped midway. Ray yanked the body down from the hideout among the stairs and threw it inside the room. He had no feeling—he was dazed. He was greatly surprised by the softness of the skin around the neck and the few strands of a woman's hair he held In his fists.

He brought the face close to his vision. The woman was still desperately clawing at his arms, but Ray was stunned. It was Rukminia. The old woman's face was flushed, her mouth was slightly apart, but she stared at him with unflinching eyes. Ray had never been able to make out the feeling that was behind the way she had always looked at him. He now felt that perhaps she was looking at someone she regarded as a despicable creature. There was not a trace of fear in her eyes; rather they expressed a fierce resolve to carry on the fight. But Ray was none too sure about that either. He was never sure what she meant. The white of her eyes glowed under the faint rays of millions of stars spread over the sky. The woman was so powerful—her body had so much strength. Ray was amazed. Ray mentally recounted a hypothetical sequence of events while he struggled with her. The warden must have wondered seeing him come out of Saxena's room with a worried look. He must have asked Rukminia, a leader of the union and the guardian angel of the worker's ghetto, to keep an eye on him. Rukminia must have been on watch not realizing what was in store for her. She must have peeped into his room at not hearing the sound of his voice, and come out to the yard not finding him there. She must have heard sounds of people moving about, or seen the torch light flickering through gaps among the sacks. But why had she come up there all by herself without bringing others along with her? Was she curious about what was going on—think she would first see for herself, then inform the others.

Ray was still grappling with the woman; he hadn't been able to bring her down. Fiercely twisting his arm, he slipped and fell backwards, and leaned against a sack as a prop. The world crumbled around him and sank into a bottomless deep, and a sound hitting against the four corners of the universe rebounded back into the room as a sharp cry! Ray went down flat on his face on the cemented floor, nudging .a whole lot of sacks to the side. He lay stunned for some time. Rukminia got on top of him, her two hands on his throat. His head throbbed amidst the swirling darkness ... Gradually Ray's nerves became calmer and feeling powerless he wrung her neck hard. His right-hand fingers which were already restlessly mobile had come into contact with the box of tools on the floor. He felt and took out a big spanner and using maximum strength brought it down on her head. She fell over the floor—a motionless body. Ray thought she had fainted as he climbed back to the window on his unsteady feet. He jutted his head out through the open window and inhaled deeply the fresh air outside. The calm of the night made his head throb less.

The night was ending and the darkness had turned fluid. Ray sat with the upper part of his body reclining against the window. He felt paralysed. After sometime he collected his tools and came below flashing his torch. There was Rukminia—sprawled on the floor—she hadn't come round. Ray went out of the place through the unlatched window and perched himself on top of the ladder. The yard was deserted. The noise of the falling sacks, that had seemed loud to his ears, hadn't travelled beyond the sealed room. He lit a match stick and held it up to survey the scene below. 'Death to her' he said to himself imagining how her body would bear the pressure of bales of cotton wool going up in flames. What did he care! At least she won't give him one of those frozen looks anymore!

He threw the match stick in ... and for the last time that night caught Rukminia's unflinching stare, in the sudden lighting up of the warehouse. She appeared fully conscious. But it was to be the last time he would be thinking about the meaning of that gaze—at least that's what he had thought.

The events that followed were simple enough. It was Ray who discovered that fire had broken out in the warehouse. He hadn't deprived himself of the pleasure of giving vent to his pent-up, mixed feelings by uttering a loud cry. He had run about like a mad man for a long time with others, trying to quench the fire. His body was covered with blisters by the time the flame was put out. The fire spared nothing, no one. The warehouse was reduced to a heap of ashes and rubble. The petrol cans hadn't attracted anyone's notice because Ray was familiar with the local authorities. A posse of police and the fire brigade helped to keep the crowds of workers at bay—the excuse that goods might disappear worked well as a deterrent.

Rukminia's dead body and the unfastened window conspired to help him construct a plausible account of the incident: it was she who had carelessly caused the fire while preparing to steal, and was, in fact, responsible for her own death in the veritable "house of wax." The insurance people, however, tried to make things difficult by raising all kinds of questions. That's why a tribunal was set up at the head office in Allahabad. Ray was summoned as the chief witness. He managed to keep the lid on the affair pretty successfully, although there were one too many loopholes in his argument. Besides Ratanlal Gupta knew how to fill up people's pockets—he had also begun to favour Ray. He buoyed Ray up with all kinds of promises apart from rewarding him with hard cash. Success seemed to be on Ray's doorstep!

Ray had got off the train at Kanpur Central in an elated mood. But come night time, his mood had changed; he started to feel bad. He had to work again in the night shift; his thoughts became more knotty as the evening deepened. He had had such a lovely time in Allahabad.

Back in the factory sitting alone in the night, he faced a troublesome situation. He found it difficult especially to look in the direction of the dark yard. He wondered why ... were his nerves playing up?

What was there on the glass surface of the table top? Were

they a pair of eyes? But how could that be ... how could those eyes appear on the glass covering his table? That was ridiculous!

A loud noise resounded in the room. Ray pounded the glass with his fists. Clerk Murari rushed in. Ray regained his composure and asked, "What do you want?" His face was turned the other way. Murari produced a sheaf of papers, "An account of the costs of production, Sir." "Come later, when there is a siren call." Ray fell over the table once more as soon as Murari left. It was there ... the pair of eyes—but wasn't it a reflection of his own eyes, his own face in the glass? He tried to rub off the image, raised his head and gave a good laugh.

The yard behind him was as dark as it had been that fateful night. The oblique rays of the sinking moon fell on the corner of the wall of the machine shop, and beyond. Ray imagined the ruins of the warehouse hid in half shadows. Nothing could be seen, yet some one stood there, gaping at him. The firm glow of a pair of eyes seemed to have gone through the thick wall and reached where he was. An unknown fear suddenly crept into his soul—a senseless, childish fear. He jumped up and ran to the doubling, passing by the Blow-room. The room, a portion of which was used for cutting was large. Fluffs of cotton were combed out there, while reels of thick cotton thread got transferred to the bobbins in the doubling section. Ray had always found the place full of workers. It looked deserted now as if it had lost its soul. The monstrous machines lay silent in the dreary emptiness. The few workers about the place looked dispirited.

Ray strolled around the machines, touching them, here and there. He inspected the revolving spindles, thrust his hand into the machine settling the spindles back into their proper places, and rolling the ends of the threads at the mouth of pipes where they had accumulated. The eyes were everywhere pursuing him still; he couldn't rest.

Srivastav was bending over a machine in one corner of the room. He was the supervisor of the operations. Ray silently crept near him; he longed for human company!

"What are you doing?" he asked.

The supervisor gave him a salute and said he was altering the count of the thread.

"Let me do that." Ray wanted to forget himself in work. So many pinions were stuck there to determine the width of the thread. He waved at the man to stop work. Srivastav closed the machine and moved to another one. Ray bent his head and asked for the spanner without lifting his face. He raised his eyes getting no response, and immediately came face to face with the operator of the machine.

It was Bhandu, Rukminia's son. A hulking youth, he was putting aside bowls of cotton thread, unmindful of his surroundings. Ray felt a strange tingling sensation all over his body. Was it fear or disgust, he wondered. There stood Rukminia's son, the son of the mother he had killed. What was he doing there? Who had given the boy the right to appear in front of him? The boy's presence would surely remind him of his mother and then those eyes would haunt him relentlessly ... Ray's whole frame shook in violent anger. Should he finish the boy off as well—oh, no!

Ray gave him a kick with his boots—"You ... bring me the spanner!" What happened next was extremely strange. The man had been working quietly, his head bent; all of a sudden he raised his hand grasping a rod. His eyes were glittering like glow worms in the dark. Ray didn't realize the boy was about to strike him; he screamed out loudly for quite another reason: the way the boy looked at him when he broke into a rage. How could the boy carry Rukminia's eyes?

Srivastav ran forward and caught Bhandu's arm and quietened him down. Along with another person, he tied him up, giving him a few blows. The incident was not uncommon. The workers became unruly from time to time.

Ray was nowhere to be seen. He had fled to the opposite end of the room. He couldn't face those eyes all over again. He slumped on the chair next to Murari's table. A panic-stricken Murari stood up. Ray forced him down on his seat like a mad man.

Andlay came running to the place hearing all the commotion. He took hold of Ray and led him into his own room. He gave him a glass of water to drink. "How are you feeling now?" he asked. "It's the after-effect of all the shock."

Ray looked at him in stunned silence, his teeth biting into his lips. His face was shiny with perspiration.

"I've asked Murari to be on guard, understand? He'll sit with you. It's five a.m., the night is almost over."

Ray didn't utter a word. Looking at him, Andlay prepared to leave, heaving a big sigh. All of a sudden Ray clutched his hand. Andlay was taken by surprise. Ray leaned forward and said in a hushed voice, "She dead. She can never come back ... what's there to be afraid of then? It's nothing!"

"There's absolutely nothing to fear," Andlay consoled him.

"No ... there is nothing. Those eyes were destroyed, they don't exist. I've nothing to be afraid of," Ray went on repeating.

Andlay finally left, removing his hand from Ray's grasp

and posting Murari next to him. Ray sat silently with his face cupped in his hands. After a while, he looked up, stared steadily at Murari, and asked. "Tell me, Murari, how can the boy have the same eyes if I have nothing to fear?"

Murari gulped a few times, "Yes sir," he said.

By then Ray was on his feet, the discomfiting feeling he had had was back. He raised his trembling hands and shouted, "Shut the door, I tell you ... that door there."

Murari went and closed the door. All of a sudden Ray gave a loud shout.

"Take hold of those eyes, Murari, catch them!"

Murari had seen him while he was closing the door. He called the man in. "What are you doing here? Come, come and show your face ..."

The man who was peering in from behind the door came forward now, looking sheepish. He was tall and thin, and had oil soaked clothes on. Ray recognized him as Jabbar Mistri who did all the fancy weaving. His eyes had a totally different aspect—they were listless and lack-luster like a dead animal's.

Murari again questioned the man's motive. In a hoarse voice, the man said he was pulverising some machine parts in the shop, he had rushed there because he had heard shouts.

Murari was about to scold him but Ray allowed the man to leave. The man left, throwing Ray a backward glance.

Murari frowned. "The fellow is the assistant secretary of the Union. I'm sure he was eavesdropping to hear what you're saying ..."

Ray made him sit down. "Come, let's talk of other things ... Do you remember our trip to Unao with the Recreation Club last year?" Ray spoke out the words in one breath. He was rolling his head furiously as if he was trying to remove something in front of his eyes: it was a pair of eyes with their corners slightly upturned, the lashes white in places; eyes dug deep with thick lines underneath; no kohl was required to make them prominent. The skin around the eyes were wrinkled. The white of the eyes had innumerable faint red lines, the pupils shone like stars—

Murari stood gaping at Ray's sleepless, blood-shot eyes, his unkempt hair, his disheveled appearance and untidy clothes. He looked stark mad! Murari tried to keep rhythm with the movement of Ray's head. He couldn't bear to see Ray's forelock waving up and down.

"Should we settle Bhandu, once and for all ..."

Ray stopped moving his head and stared at Murari. His lips were slightly apart; his brows raised in a peculiar pose, his eyes looked ferocious. Murari felt frightened; he stopped asking questions. Ray spoke in a thin voice, "What were you saying, Murari?"

"We've decided to hand Bhandu over to the police," Murari began unenthusiastically. "The way he raised his hands he would have committed a terrible crime. But some workers have raised an objection. They would like to inform the union. Unless we teach these people a lesson, Sir ..."

"Isn't it the beginning of dawn," Ray interrupted.

"Yes, Sir."

Ray made some silent calculations, and all at once became cheerful. "Once the day breaks there will be nothing to fear. Those eyes will disappear. I will myself realise that those eyes were the product of my stupid imagination, won't I?"

Murari had to agree though he could hardly fathom what

Ray meant. Ray sat happily looking at the walls in front of him with steady eyes. Murari was uncomfortable sitting face to face with his superior.

The six o'clock siren unsettled the thin morning air. The main switch in the transformer room was shut off. The machines inside the factory grindingly came to a halt. There was only the noise of shuffling feet, of human voices, and the movement of goods. Murari got up with sleepy eyes. "Sir, the siren has gone."

"What! So we must leave now? Come, let's go," Ray stuttered, rapidly rolling his eyes.

Murari came out with Ray. His duty would end after he handed Ray over to Andlay. They came through the inner gate and were dumbstruck. The main gate was locked. People, finishing work, had assembled there. They could hear the shouts of voices in the street outside, as if a crowd had gathered there—a crowd of agitated human beings.

Ray laughed, "The street is flooded with daylight ... let's go out," he said. Murari gulped a few times while Ray strode to the front gate thrusting his hands into his pockets. The workers stood aside to make room for him. But only the watch and the guard of the main gate gave a silent salute and hung about nonchalant. Andlay had come out of his office by that time, and had seen Murari. He asked in a low voice, "Where is he ... For heaven's sake, take him inside!"

Andlay got worried when Murari pointed to Ray—he ran towards the gate. Ray was ordering the guard to open the gate, and the guard was telling him he had to keep it shut as there were masses of people outside. There could be trouble.

Ray kept shouting, "Open the gate, I tell you ..."

Andlay quickly caught hold of his hands. "Look Ray, trouble is brewing! Take the manhole door and get out fast. Go straight to your bungalow; I'll join you soon."

Ray turned his crazy eyes on Andlay, "You don't understand ...all the light, the air outside. I felt suffocated inside the mill—what are you upto? Open the gate," he shouted to the gate keeper.

The watch and wardman turned the key into the lock. Andlay was stunned. Ray had become mad, a lunatic. He was looking at Andlay, gesturing with his hands and laughing his heart out, uttering: "its daylight!" Andlay swiftly held him and pulled him back. The gate came ajar making Andlay abruptly give up. The sun had just begun to shine, and was brightening up the heads and bodies of the workers of the factory of the industrial city of Kanpur, whose sky remained permanently overcast with a pall of smoke, issuing continuously from the rows of chimneys. The workers stood gazing at Ray with a silent determination. The fancy weaver, Jabbar, was among the assembled men; his hand was raised—his finger pointed at Ray.

Ray started with fear. He wasn't worried about all the people, but what he saw in those eyes—eyes belonging to all the men assembled there now. Rukminia's eyes had proliferated and spread among them.

And it also seemed that their significance had at last dawned on Ray. Those eyes carried the weight of accountability. Ray would be pulled away and torn to pieces to 'square things up.' Rukminia's eyes had hinted at the 'squaring up'. Andlay's heart missed a couple of beats at Ray's piercing cry. Ray's eyes looked as if they had got dislodged from their sockets; his screaming didn't seem to come to an end.

The hand didn't move; it pointed unwaveringly at Ray. It was a sign of what was inevitable, and it had the support of so many pairs of eyes. Thousands of replicas of Rukminia's eyes were gazing at him quietly, unflinchingly. They were coming dangerously close. Ray's small world was getting smaller, obscured by the gaze of so many eyes like Rukminia's.

Ray turned back and ran, making an ugly sound. The eyes pursued him, dogged his footsteps, closed in, shadowed his path. But Ray wanted to escape the piercing look, get away from it all.

Why must his life be spoilt by those eyes?

1949

Comrade

Jhabbu appeared at the turning of Panrre's pan shop; I quickly made myself invisible behind the tree. I didn't want him to see me. Jhabbu was walking my way at great speed, casting panicky glances everywhere. For a while he stopped to wipe his neck. I could see, even at this distance that his hands were shaking. He came along this side and went over to the raised platform facing the slums, past the tree behind which I was hiding. The doors of most of the slum hutments were shut. People inside them might have been lying prostrate—depressed and discouraged by the turn of events. Many had left the place; even the pariah dogs had gone elsewhere in search of their livelihood. There were no sounds of crying children. The place looked dark and deserted, silent—despite the presence of human beings.

Jhabbu was my dear friend and the much loved hero of our union of combatting workers. He was a companion in my joy and sorrow. I noticed him entering his room glancing at the slum with startled eyes. I heard his door shut in the tranquility of the late evening. I emerged from my hiding place still carrying the bundle of clothes—the velvet head gear, wife's flowery saree, other things—my wife had pressed into my hand. I was taking them to Lakshmi Marwari's shop in the central market to sell. Jhabbu's sudden appearance upset my plans.

I had seen Jhabbu crossing the threshold of the front door and entering the large new house of Srivastav, the owner of the factory. I had seen two other persons with him who I knew. One of them was a new recruit to the recently formed union of the puppets of the establishment; the other, Nanda Mistri, was a favourite informer of the manager and an expert in placing the blame on others. Taken by fright I had come out of the shop and had hurried towards them in case Jhabbu needed my help—Why were those two taking Jhabbu along with them—I wondered. But as I came near I found Jhabbu laughing—happiness writ large on his face. I was stunned, made an about turn and ran back to my place. I couldn't make sense of what I had seen. All my calculations had gone wrong; I felt pangs of uneasiness.

Climbing onto the platform I went near his room now. The forlorn look of the slums and the fastened doors made me want to weep. The forty-one-day lockout had drawn a pall of gloom over the place. The establishment had tried, by whatever means they could muster, to weaken the workers' united resistance; they hadn't succeeded. The workers had gone back to their villages. So many of them had had to sell all their belongings to scratch up half a meal a day; 'great hunger' had loomed over hundreds of households but the revolutionary spirit of those men had remained unwavering even to this day. The establishment wanted to keep the factory open with the help of a group of sycophants, but the new recruits were too scared to carry out the bosses' wishes. The owner had also declared he didn't care about making profits and could close the factory down if things got out of hand. He had threatened to hire labourers from Bilaspur or some such place to keep the factory running; he had once even tried to create trouble by letting loose a gang. But we have stayed firm and have remained unbending, contemptuously brushing aside all such provocations.

I felt pained and agitated at the thought of the indescribable hardships our martyrs had had to bear while they inched towards their own death. Their infinite resolve to resist and to continue their 'day and night' struggle had made them turn their faces away from the sight of their dying beloved ones and wipe away their tears. There was not another example of fortitude in adversity in the entire world. There was nothing nobler in life than these bands of revolutionaries.

I came and stood in front of the door of Jhabbu's room. Not a sound could be heard—as if no one lived inside. There was no light in the room either, although not many people could afford the luxury of electricity. I couldn't hear his voice, so I knocked. Sounds of footsteps rose from within—the latch was lifted ... Jhabbu unfastened the door. He was our leader still, a warrior of the oppressed classes. His face turned ash-coloured when he saw me. Why was that? Wasn't he the same Jhabbu, and me? Was I not merely a hungry, destitute factory worker?—Why had he become pale at my sight?

Jhabbu forced a smile. "Come in Lalbahadur, come right in. How is it you are here today?" His voice sounded dull and unenthusiastic. He moved his hand away from the door, and pointed to the dirty, soiled bed. The dull gray room gave out a suffocating smell. The extreme poverty of the surroundings hit me hard.

"Sit," he said, "let me light the lamp ... I've done away with all that you know!"

I tried to stop him. "Let go of it. We don't need any light ... let's sit together."

I sat on the bed with the bundle next to me. He went on fingering his shirt pocket, distinctly restless. "Have a bidi."

"I may, thanks." I said.

I held the bidi close to my mouth and bent my head down, while he struck a match to light his. He brought the flame near my face and I saw his eye balls glinting like two bright flames, although his eyes had a dull and despairing look. I went on staring at him, sticking my head out. He felt uncomfortable and looked the other way, gradually fixing his gaze outside the open window above my head.

I lifted my face and asked, "So you still have money to buy bidis?"

"I don't," he threw the match stick on the floor. "I don't know why I had this sudden urge to smoke today."

"Well!" I blew out a ring of smoke, "Where are the kids and your wife? I don't hear any voices!"

"Oh that ... I've packed them off to the village this morning. Who knows how long the lockout will last. There, at least, they can have two square meals a day. And what about you? You've hardly been around the past two days—what brings you here now?"

"I'll tell you," I said, carefully calculating how much information I ought to reveal—So the scene I had been witness to that afternoon was not just a flash in the pan, but a part of an ongoing conspiracy—Jhabbu had become weak-kneed since the birth of his last child—He had sent his wife away because he anticipated trouble.

"Ahmad Sahab is arriving tomorrow," I spoke out. "The union got the information this morning. You've been avoiding the office for so many days ... all the arrangements for the visit have to be made."

Jhabbu hesitated. "I haven't been well for some time; I don't go out at all. I had to take my wife and son to the station this morning. I've had to sell all my possessions to find money for their trip—know that? One needs money as soon as one goes out of the house."

"Then why do you have your shirt on, sitting indoors?" I asked.

"Oh! Just like that." He looked at me worried. "I had been thinking about going out ... It's so suffocating sitting here alone.

"Is that so?" I pretended my curiosity was satisfied. "But ... when did you buy the bidis, brother?" I asked.

Jhabbu gave a start; he straightened up. "In the morning when I put my wife on the train ... why do you ask?"

I didn't give a reply, but quietly inspected his face. He wasn't able to gather enough courage to be downright rude to me. All of a sudden he got up and poured a glass of water from the pitcher, hidden among the shadows in the corner of the room, and gulped it down. I stubbed the bidi underfoot as he came towards me.

"I've come because we have to arrange a meeting for Ahmad Sabah ... only you can do the job." I said.

"A meeting? Ah yes, of course we'll have to bring all the people here. But Lalbahadur I must tell you something." He leaned forward.

"Shoot off," I said, "Jhabbu! you are our only recourse when the workers become weak with no food in their stomachs. You are the only person they will listen to, no one else, brother!" Jhabbu controlled his excitement and remained silent.

"What was it you were about to tell me?" I asked.

He gave me a look from out of the corner of his eye and said calmly, "Lalbahadur you are my best friend ... but leave that for the present. I have something to say as a fellow comrade."

I didn't interrupt him.

"I know that the workers trust me; they will understand what I have to tell them. They will see my point ..."

Wasn't it that what I feared most? What was, ironically, the source of my pride and joy in him. An oblique brightness fell on the floor like a dot of light. Someone in the second story building had put the light on. Jhabbu went on talking. The eager, beseeching tone of his voice, next to my ears, made me feel sick. "Look at the hutments ... I have gone around all of them. What a derelict state they've been reduced to! There's a limit to human endurance."

"What is it you want to say?" I asked, indifferent.

"That this state of affairs can't go on forever ... I have no right to drag people into this miserable condition. The factory closed down because I gave a strike call. I can't carry the burden of so many people's lives any more ... that's why I say ... let's try to find a solution; let's talk to our bosses, tell them about our demands."

A segment of light now filtered through the window. It fell on his cheeks how sharp and protruded his cheek bones had become, how pinched his face, how sunk his eyes Jhabbu had become so skinny!—

"Solution?" I jeered, you mean compromise, and you suggest that?" I was furious. But to my ears, my own voice sounded like the faint rumble of a distant thunder.

"Don't take it that way ... I think, in fact I know, they will accede to our demands. Then there would be no point in carrying on this agitation."

"How do *you* know that?" I talked fast looking straight at him.

He bit his tongue in embarrassment. "That's what I think ..." His voice had lost some of its ardour.

"Would they give back jobs to those they have sacked, like Prakash Bhaiya? Increase the salaries of the workers? Will they agree to all these?"

Jhabbu thought for a while. "We can try ... I do think they will respect some of our demands.

"Some?" I repeated outraged, my desire to carry on the conversation eroding fast.

"I can't bear to see people die by inches—think of that! We will tell Ahmad Sahab about our decision tomorrow, let the crowd know what we think when they assemble here. We must go back to work!"

I was livid. "You want to destroy what we have built with our blood over the years: our strength in our unity? You want to strike at the root of our resistance, interfere with our onward course?" I blurted out.

"No, you misunderstand me ..." He took on a conciliatory tone. "The fight must go on; we'll be in the battle field again! But let's pause a while now to recover our breath; give up a little so that so many lives may be saved."

He made an eye contact with me. My eyes must have been shouldering. He said in a pathetic voice, "How can you talk to me like this ... you are such a dear friend—the love we have had for each other for so many years ..."

"Love!" I wanted to scream—Jhabbu my comrade in arms, the pride of our revolutionary band; at least that was how he was regarded by all of us. No one was privy as yet to my newly gained wisdom. The workers were still mad about him—Jhabbu perhaps noticed me looking tender; he rested his hand on my arm. I shivered at his touch, but didn't push his hand away.

"Brother ... please understand," he implored, "I'm asking you to give a serious thought to my proposal."

His voice became faint as it entered my ears. I was thinking of all the past events: Jhabbu's thundering call to protest whenever the machinery of oppression began to grind us down. His image would send us into a rapture, and we became oblivious of the world around us. He was truly inspired by an inner sacrificial urge; he wouldn't take a mean step or make unholy compromises. How was it that the same person had grown so weak now? How could a veteran soldier who had passed through the ordeal of so many battles lose his mettle? Had Jhabbu sold his soul for filthy lucre; had he fallen so low?

I wanted to clasp him in my arms and weep. I gripped his hands and said, "Have you taken leave of your senses that you no longer know what is good and what is bad for us? Think hard ...

a compromise now will mean sure death, an end to all our hopes. Abandon this kind of thinking ... what will all the workers say?"

"All the workers?" Jhabbu turned his gaze away from me and fixed it on the dark. He looked as if his mind was made up. "We'll have to compromise ... I have been your leader for so many years. You must trust me."

"Leader!" The word fell on my face like a whip. Was that his final argument? I was beside myself with anger. I was mad. What an astounding revelation! My heart was heavy with sorrow. The ground under my feet began to shift, the atmosphere was turning incredibly murky. And I realised that the suspicion I had vaguely entertained in my mind when I came across him in the main market square, late afternoon was indeed true. it was disgusting!

Jhabbu continued to blabber, but now I was no longer interested in his talk. Who cares about the ghost-speak of a dead man! I regretted he was not killed in the disturbances that had taken place some time back. He had braved the enemy's bullet when the workers came to blows with their bosses. Why hadn't a bullet pierced his body then, and finished him off? Why had he to live?

I didn't wish him ill; I had never thought of anything harmful for him. But I couldn't help feeling it would have been better for him to have died. We could have gone on a procession carrying his corpse on our shoulders, tears raining down our cheeks. Jhabbu would have become immortal, caught in each tear we shed, transforming our sorrow into resolve. He would have remained alive in our hopes, in our defeats, and in our improbable, but certain victory at the end. His thought would have given us comfort in our calamity, strength in our fight. His image would have spurred us on to face sure annihilation. His example would have drawn the youth to our cause, and roused revolutionary fire in their hearts. When after many a battle we would build the foundation of a just society, his memory would have remained with us, like a waft of hope in the air, in the smile lighting up the faces of innumerable peasants and workers. He would have become eternised in our thoughts as Jhabbu the great, who had given his life in the people's cause!

But the man who was in front of me, who called himself a leader ... how could he possibly be one of us? He was cast in a different mould. His eyes belied fear; he was ever-ready to turn any situation to his own advantage; his pockets were stuffed with cash. A fragment of light from the outside shone on his jaw bones; it was in continuous motion. There wasn't another perfidious being like him in this world; didn't I know that? He was my enemy number one. *My* Jhabbu's eternal foe, the mercenary leader of thousands of famished workers.

Jhabbu was demonstrating loudly, gesturing with his hands; I was sitting motionless as a pillar. I stirred myself. My favourite velvety-soft head gear came unrolling in my hands. Jhabbu *was* my friend, the greatest friend I had ever had. I had fought for our cause under his leadership. I was indebted to him in so many different ways. I began to weaken ... felt I wasn't up to the job. Perhaps it were better to have left straightaway. Why did I have to come to him? My head was heavy. I pressed my lips hard and swallowed the tears that were welling up in my eyes. My lips quivered.

His voice choked in the middle of a sentence. The night deepened.

I wound the cloth several times tightly around his neck using all my strength. His head lolled perilously close to my face. His tongue hung out. Drops of sweat covered his forehead; his eyes were bloodshot. Once more I pulled the noose around the neck, and saw his limbs go limp. He still clutched on to a portion of my shirt; it made a tearing sound. I watched the entire proceeding as if through a dark red screen. I felt I was a detached impersonal observer of events. I felt nothing.

His body rolled over. His hands and feet stopped moving. His head fell on my lap. In the light streaming through the open window his face looked as if it no longer bore any trace of agony; the portion of the shirt that had covered my chest was still locked in his grip.

I removed the cloth around his neck at one go, and looked at the flock of hair on his forehead—his broad front covered with drops of white perspiration. He looked so calm and contented as if he was slowly sinking into a deep sleep.

I kept bending over his body, my face wet with tears. My hands shook as with utmost love I brushed aside the forelock which hid his face.

1949

The Road[1]

Sarak

The road lies in between pavements on its either side. The sun's rays roast its smooth, well-upholstered black-tarred surface. Leaves of shady trees cast a spell of latticework overhead. It is high noon. Two corresponding tall flowering red *krishnachura trees*, poised against the pavement, face the dilapidated buildings in the front; the two huge trees reach out to each other from either side of the road in a fierce embrace of love, and form an immense archway. The vault of sunshine-tinted, tender green leaves, soothing to the eye, sways at the bidding of the wind. The lattice work of light and shade overhead awakens to its rhythm. Srr ... srr ... Such a sweet sound they make! The road lies still, as if resigned.

On the pavement opposite are the blackened, broken-down, hollowed-out empty houses and shops—the wreckage of a devastated tradition. There was an unnamed slum there

1. 'This is a modified version of the translation which first appeared in the anthology of Bangla short stories, *Homes in Emptiness*, 2000.

once. Now the street is totally deserted; only at times one hears muffled noises of some people. Human voices, hushed further by the feeble wind, enter the ear in this empty landscape.

I don't know why we both decided to come and sit by the side of this pavement when we suddenly found ourselves free one afternoon. My friend sat next to me in silence. He got furious when I said, "My dear Israel used to live in one of the rooms belonging to this slum ... let's go and see him since we've come thus far." I was talking unnecessarily, he remarked.

I caught on ... I know my friend only too well; he is so tender-hearted. A burden of sorrow weighs heavily permanently on his head. I cannot make him understand that the tears of people, crossing the borders in bands, spreading out in our towns and outskirts, have turned our country into a sleeping volcano. He gets angry if I say that, but it is all there for us to see how the seeds of flaming fury are being sown.

He sees only the tragedy, this friend of mine!

It was he who brought me here today, to this side of the street. I had come here so many times when Israel used to live here. Emdad was his son. And what a son! What a fierce desire to paint the boy had had! And my friend—he had fuelled that desire; brought him colourful chalks. The boy had enthusiastically traced lines all over the walls and the floor with them. One can't keep track of the countless lashings the boy had to endure at the hands of Israel because of it. At one point Israel almost came to blows with my friend for encouraging such waywardness. But what a lot of talent the boy had! Who knows what he might have become! Who bothers about these things?

I will not see all those familiar faces today. I don't know where Israel and his family have fled. Now I see a new group of people take possession of his home. Who has brought these people over here? Are they those who would gain by misdirecting their anger. And do they know that hunger is a great teacher—the more one burns in hunger the more one is reduced to fodder, waiting to be consumed by fire.

My friend snapped at my comment.

"What a lot of bunkum! Hearing you talk like this one would think you are happy at their plight; at least those who don't know you are bound to think that way."

How long can I go on playing along with his strange eccentricities? I was about to get up when a surprising thing happened. I saw Israel; actually both of us saw him, almost at once.

I had never in my dreams thought I would find Israel there this very day. He didn't look at all surprised seeing us. He came to us straightaway.

He had dark rings under his eyes; his hair had bleached to a blond colour; his big fat cheeks seemed as if they had caved in. He was staring at the slum with blazing eyes.

My friend asked, "So you haven't gone ... as yet?"

Israel's attention was riveted to a room.

He grunted between his teeth. "That's the room I stayed in ... do you know? I have spent sixteen years of my life inside it.

My friend repeated his question. "Why haven't you left?"

"I will now. I had thought where can I go ... I don't know anyone in *that* country. I had to go to Park Circus; I am ready to leave now.

He sat holding his breath. We both remained silent. The leafy fringe overhead swayed to and fro. One or two persons came out from the other side of the road, one or two others went in. Each face had a history of its own.

Israel started to talk again. "Do you remember my boy Emdad ... remember him?"

Yes we did! A head covered with a thick mop of hair, a naughty smile spread all over his face ... how could one forget the boy? I glanced at my friend. He was sitting, face down, scratching the dirt with a bit of a stick. Israel continued, "It was all over for him last night you know. Emdad died of cholera at the Park Circus refugee camp last night."

The corner of his eyes appeared a little red. He stared at us.

"Why did he have to die—can you tell me? No, you can't!"

He started every now and then while he fixed a harsh gaze on us. Then he looked downwards. My friend appeared very disconcerted. He moved restlessly a few times and said, "Israel, why don't you ... for a few days, I mean ..."

"*Khamosh!*" Israel thundered. "You can't console me with your snivelling sorrow. Who do you take me for? Know who am?

He gaped at us, turned his face away with a jerk, then took a few firm steps only to stop all of a sudden in his tracks. I went near and stood behind him and asked, "Have you eaten anything? Had some food during the day?"

He shook his blond hair covered with dust.

"Want to eat?" I asked again.

He turned around. His eyes were brimming with tears.

"Something is going wrong inside my head, *Ostad*."

I touched him. He grasped my hand, pressed it twice over, then walked by my side with an embarassed smile—like some rain-smudged sky—on his face. We sat at the corner sweet shop, the three of us, and ate.

Israel was eating mechanically without uttering a word. My friend was looking at him taking fistfuls of food. He turned his face away as soon as his eyes met mine. Israel got up to wash his hands when he finished eating. Panic-stricken my friend moved his chair and made way for him. The legs of the chair grazed the floor and made an ugly sound. Israel stood up, gave us both a strange look and parted his lips slightly.

"*Dost*," he said.

My friend became joyous on his own. He threw Israel a caressing look. We paid for our food and left.

Again we arrived at the pavement and the leafy vault. Not a leaf moved now in the scorching afternoon sun. The wretched sky, covered with a fine film of smoke, looked coppery.

Someone was lying against a pillar on the other side. We could see his back. He was singing indifferently and out of tune even before we had got there.

O you boat of my soul, driven by desire!

Go to the country where lives the radiant beauty!

The song lightened my friend's mood. He spoke out happily.

"That's what I like about the *Bangals* ... they sing so well!"

Israel had again shut up. He kept on looking at the slums. He said, "Listen to me Babu, I'll speak the truth. Damn it—that was *my* room! I had spent all this time there. Today someone comes and occupies it; won't I get angry? Feel like finishing off the bastard? But I know there's no justice in this place. That's why I am leaving for Pakistan. That room, this road, you and so much else ... won't my heart break to leave all this behind? But I need a place to live; that's why I must go."

"Who stays in the place now?" my friend asked.

"Who knows? Whoever he may be I will find no peace until I can tear him to pieces. He is my enemy now—the whole country is my enemy."

Suddenly my friend spoke out like a sage.

"Who's the enemy—that's the problem."

The dissonant strains of the song, like the sound of wailing, floated in through the gaps of their conversation. My friend stopped talking and listened. He heaved a deep sigh. "The songs are good, really! One tends to become soulful listening to them.

Israel slapped his knee and got up; he walked a few steps without speaking a word. He stopped and turned his head to have a look and found us staring at him. He talked to himself as if he were answering someone, "No! Emdad was such an expert in pulling off pictures—a big expert! They have destroyed everything but they couldn't erase his signature on the wall—the picture of his *Nanijan* on the mud wall. And how I thrashed him for drawing something that day! A railway perhaps. He used red, green and yellow coloured chalks ... was a great friend of yours, wasn't he?"

He was looking at us with his mouth wide open.

A trace of a shy smile played around his eyes.

My friend spoke out slowly. "Emdad drew beautiful pictures."

Israel's facial expression gradually altered. He turned his gaze, absentmindedly, first at my friend and then at the slum. Anxiety had cast dream-like shadows over his eyes. He had totally forgotten our existence; he turned and left the place.

The youth, who was singing, was flat out under the shade of a tree; he had stopped crooning. The sun was travelling westward; the afternoon running its full course was coming to an end.

"That'll be all," I said. "But tell me why have we come here at all ... why do we keep sitting? I don't understand any of this!"

My friend gave me a look from out of the corner of his eye. He was squatting, swinging his body to and fro, etching diagrams on the dust. He wrote "Israel", put a bold full stop after it, and held up his hands. "I had wanted to see Israel very much ... after all this time," he said. "I wanted to visit his locality, at least. Tell me what a long time it's been since we were here last. We hadn't thought of him even once in all the confusion."

I began to feel uncomfortable. I didn't see any sense in spending an entire afternoon sitting like this. I will get a headache in the stifling heat, I thought. All of a sudden my friend asked, "Tell me one thing, *Ostad* ..."

"What is it?"

"What did you think of his son, Emdad?"

"Unforgettable! He would have turned into a great artist one day!"

"Wouldn't he have?" my friend directed his curious eyes at me.

"No, perhaps he wouldn't have ... perhaps he would have packed *bidis* or something like that."

"Ok. *Ostad*," he said, his head aslant, his brows puckered, looking up at the sky.

"Say what you have to."

"Emdad is dead. He will be placed inside a coffin and laid on the ground. He's gone for good. There's nothing left of him—wouldn't you say?"

I looked at him; I was silent!

"He won't demand chalks of us—won't ask anything of anyone. All his cravings have come to an end. And won't our desires too ... come to an end one day. Mine as well?"

"Yes, but what of that?" I asked.

"Well, I was thinking about the man who is singing—he was. He's lying down now. He too must have come from a place known to him. The people there won't hear his songs anymore ... a day will come when none will be left there to hear him. The language of desire of those songs will cease to have any meaning at all."

I couldn't gauge what he was getting at although he continued talking as if to himself.

"That means death brings an end to all our yearnings, longings of the soul, our appetites ... all of these. Now I want to say something ... see if it makes any sense. If those who can fulfill our desires don't do that, what could they be wanting? That we die? All of us die with our songs and pictures? An end to all the bother ... what do you say?"

I didn't think in the same vein. My friend had woven his web of argument with too fine a thread. I remained quiet.

He went on. "We are all dying today ... will die, no doubt. That means some people want us dead. Who are they? Those who have the capacity to give us what we want? That is so. I mean ... oh dear!"

I looked up hearing him exclaim. He was standing looking up at the sky. I too turned my gaze upwards. Small black clouds were crawling slowly from a corner of the western horizon, advancing to fill up the entire upper atmosphere which had turned coppery in the haze of a thin smoke. From time to time a flash of lightning lit up the folds of the clouds. A suppressed roar, like some tiger about to spring on its prey, came from afar. My eyes felt cool, soothed by the signs of the rejuvenating rain.

My friend sat inert, sunk in the shadows of despair. I felt disheartened by his attitude. Suddenly he gave my hand a pull—spoke out! with a hushed excitement in his voice. "*Ostad*!"

"What is it?"

He looked conspiratorially at me for a while and said, "Shall we go and see Emdad's handiwork? Come let's." He pulled me along with him without waiting for a reply.

The familiar room in the slum. The little lane was deserted for all to see. We heard voices as soon as we turned the corner. We looked ahead. My friend's eyes opened wide in surprise. We didn't go any further. They hadn't seen us, Israel and the old woman. She was old no doubt, with a face creased like a shrivelled up ripe mango. Looking at her two eyes, I suddenly felt dejected remembering the strong breeze of the big Padma river. She was wiping her nose again and again with the end of her dirty saree *anchal*. Her red-bordered saree declared her married woman status. There was a faint trace of *sindoor* on her forehead.

A room that *was* Israel's. Its walls were covered with Emdad's handiwork. Israel was sweeping his own room, gathering all the dust in a paper. The woman was sitting with her feet rested on the threshold. She was gazing at him.

"I have arranged all your belongings, cleaned your room," Israel was telling her, "Now enter the house. Why keep on sitting like this?" The old woman spoke out falteringly, "You have done me a great favour, son. Yes, my hips are broken. I don't have the strength to do any work now. But I had a lot of ability once. The prosperous world of Satkhani village knew this Brahmin woman by name ... whether it was the *puja* season, festival time or a ceremonial occasion, it was I who was there. People would say that Jagat Brahmini woman has ten hands, like the goddess Durga, so ..."

"Your room looks fine, let me go now." Israel promptly declared. The old woman looked at him strangely and laughed. She looked down. "Look what a state I am reduced to ... driven by want." She lifted her face. "You haven't offered me any food son, I am so hungry."

"Ah yes," Israel felt ashamed. "I mean ... I have no money with me. Will you come outside? My friends are stopping by the road. I will have to ask them for some."

"Let's go. I can't do without food. I have no money, no rice. My grandson is running after some mirage ... such a song-crazy boy!"

The old woman got up. She asked Israel not to shut the front door.

"Where's the need to bolt the door," she said. "I haven't a penny to my name. And what else is there?"

Israel noticed some discoloration on the shutter as he was about to fasten the chain. He ran his fingertips over it. Someone, long ago, had tried his hand at drawing a human face. He turned to the woman and said, as if in a trance, "Even so we can't leave your room unlocked." There was a strange look in his eyes—I could see it, even from such a distance.

The old woman screwed her face. "Dear me ... is this my room? I have been telling you, son, the room is not to my liking.

O what a wonderful door the room had! Decorated all over with lotus flower-like designs! What a fantastic courtyard! How can I make you understand what my home looked like? Who is there for me to tell?"

"Ok, ok, let's go now." Israel held her carefully and led her on.

The old woman took one step and gave him a big stare. "Son! looking at you another person comes to my mind—Who was it who held me like this? Who?"

"Good, let's go now," Israel hurried her. It seemed that he couldn't bear to look at her anymore. Coming forward he came face to face with us. A big animal that he was, he appeared shrunk in embarrassment now. She looked up, and leaned back against his wide chest. And he, inadvertently, removed his hands from the old woman's shoulders.

"They are my friends," Israel assured her while he turned to us. "What made you come here?"

My friend went forward. "Here, take the money."

Israel came to me. My friend grinned, giving me a knowing look. A smile also played around the old woman's toothless gums. It seemed as if a gush of cool air like flash had penetrated the hopelessly suffocating atmosphere. My friend was an expert in making friends. He followed behind keeping the old woman's company.

When we were back on the road, Israel said in a hushed voice.

"Forgive me friend. Hadn't I said that I would find no peace till I tear to bits the person who lives in my room now? Did I know then that this wretched old woman would be there?"

The road led us straight to the archway of trees.

Israel continued. "The old woman has a grandson, a youth of sixteen years. A family of eighteen have got scattered and destroyed. Some have died, others have fled no one knows where. Only these two have come and got stuck here. They don't want to stay. They had a house somewhere on the banks of the river Padma ... that's ..." He stopped, looked about the place. There was such compassion all over Israel's face. He looked so handsome! As if all the beauty of this wide world was gathered there, on his eyes and face. His heart seemed overflowing with love.

Faint strains of music were coming from afar; I found that the youth, still lying on his back, had once again picked up the thread of his song: "*O you boat of my soul, driven by desire ...*" My friend along with the old woman reached where we were. They had struck up a great friendship already.

"Where was your home, Ma?"

"O dear! that's the question. Isn't it? Can you tell me where is my home ... you can't. It is tied up in a labyrinth. That's it ..." She giggled without completing the sentence.

"O where is that pretty house next to the river Padma? Who will take me there?"

Israel and my friend exchanged glances. Israel asked, "What does your grandson do?"

"Sing." She shut her eyes. "He sang very well. He sang so many songs, so many songs! Can't you hear? There ..."

We were all ears. The song had come alive in his youthful voice. Although heard from afar it came through to us, strong and clear. He sang:

The river is red where rises the red sun
Blushing with love at the red sky

Follow the course of the red river as it flows into its estuary
O you boat of my soul, driven by desire.

The singer repeated the first line of the song, over and over again; the emotions, condensed in his young heart, cascaded, and the abounding generosity of the Padma river carried aloft by the strains of that melody entered our souls while we stood under the red-streaked sky.

The old woman spoke out, "Dear sons, you have forgotten the important thing—where's the food?"

"Ah! Yes," Israel held his breath. "Give me some money *Ostad*."

I fingered my pocket and took out a few coins. Israel left for the sweet shop. My friend and the woman sat down side by side. I kept on looking.

How the old woman could talk ... so much in one breath! My friend was sitting and scratching his feet while I listened. An image of a village began to form in my mind's eye. She herself created the image—herself laughed at all that. Her eyes were wet and she sat still. Israel turned up with food in a packet made out of *sal* leaves in the midst of all this. The woman ate some of the food and tied up the rest in her *anchal*, for her grandson perhaps. She was an addict all right; she took out some tobacco from a loop and thrust it into her mouth; then resumed her narrative. Neither irritated nor fatigued, she continued with the story of her home. Her grandson had a similar enthusiasm for singing songs about the Padma—of that I had no doubt.

It was so far away ... none of us had been to that country which was her home ... where the evening lamp was lit under the *tulsi* tree on the clay-coated courtyard every evening ... where the acrid *chalta* fruit tree stood, overlooking the scene. The woman got excited describing her favourite tree standing at the corner of a clump of bamboos. The smell of damp, rotten leaves would enter the nose, darkness hover thickly, and a ring of shadow from mango and jackfruit trees fall around the patch of land where it stood. She exclaimed, "O dear! What a tree it is; must be laden with fruit now ... hanging suspended with no one to see or hear. Night birds may be coming and sitting on its branches in the deep of night, flapping their wings; fruit may be falling on the ground—plong, plong. And I too could hear, clearly, sounds of that night—hear *chalta* fruit ripen and fall. How much do they cost in Calcutta now?

Suddenly, the woman looked up. Black amorphous clouds had almost covered the reclining afternoon sky. The shape of the clouds could hardly be seen, spread as they were over the entire horizon. The clouds came in big waves, like armed soldiers, making the sky reverberate with a warlike, thunderous noise. Lightning played all over the place, streaking the folds.

The woman sat, resting her cheek on the palm of her hand.

"O dear! It's *Kalbaisakhi*! The Nor'wester is coming thick and fast! The dears! take me into my room. Take me in."

Israel got up and led her a few steps; then seeing my friend sitting like a zombie, tried to say something. He hesitated, tried again to lead the woman to her room. The woman's grandson kept singing without pause. I said, "Come on now, get up. It will rain; what's the point in sitting?"

"Uhmm." My friend looked absentminded. "Ok. let's go."

He got up and took my hand in a firm grasp; excited, he said, "Good ... let's do something; let's go to the houses of all our friends—we have not a few of them—and bring them together to this situation ..." He paused, worried. "I mean something will come of it. I can't explain ... but there must be a way."

He probably didn't find his own arguments weighty enough; he scratched his head.

"I am at the end of my tether with ideas crawling in my head," he said. "*Ostad* isn't there a way to attain freedom from all our wants? I don't know ..."

He got disheartened. But I was quite elated by then. The ensemble of clouds that seemed stationary, as if sitting in council, rushed and kissed me now. I felt the lashings of a moist breeze—The twist and turn of the song could still be heard. We left the history-encrusted pavement behind, and came and stood on the well-padded road; it was scalding in the heat. We moved out into the open from under the protection of the leafy arch. Daylight had become dim beneath the veil of descending clouds. But there was a hint of brightness lurking everywhere, like the glint of well-polished copper *vessels*.

Then the rains came.

It fell in torrents drowning the lone youth's voice with its sound. I felt as if his song had been taken up by millions of voices now!

My friend was happy with the rain splashing all over his hot, tired, perspiring body. Water streamed down his nose, his face, and he sucked some of it with his lips, making a sound.

The sky rang loudly; the earth reverberated with music. Glancing behind, my friend exclaimed, "Look, look!"

What could I possibly see? I turned round. The leaves of the red-flowering *krishnachura* tree were bobbing up and down; flowers were frolicking. The sorrows of human beings seemed to have got transformed, and had become heroic against the white sheet of rain. Exulting in happiness, my friend ran his fingers through his hair; patted them on his forehead. Some water fell. He cried out, "Can't you see—can't you hear? Put your ears to the ground."

He bent down on his knees, pressed his ears against the road, then craned his neck, and beheld me.

"See ... I can hear so many people marching, taking strong strides! And you laugh? Why not lend your ears ... your ears! You talk utter rubbish."

Heavy drops of rain bounced and rebounded back on the road. I too pressed my ear to the ground, to give them company.

Goom, goom, goom, goom, goom, goom, goom, goom.

The pulsating throb of millions on the march!

1954

Love

Prem

He came. The colossal crest of the tamal tree, facing him, convulsed like one possessed, in the unruly storm. Next to it, the betel tree kept hitting the ground.

Nose, eyes and ears were getting choked by dust lifted from the banks. The river Padma in the winter! The wind made such a distinctly delightful sound; one could appreciate the peculiar nature of the river breeze only if one sat on its shore on a full-moon-lit night.

He appeared in the middle of it all.

It's difficult to explain the meaning of his arrival. He was a boy who would sit by the brink of the Padma river and gaze at the land, which was not always visible, looming on the other side. The clouds across the river would appear like shrines of faraway places. He would listen to the sound of conch-shells, breathe in the scent of glowing joss sticks and get mesmerised. He arrived there now, in a state that was all too familiar to us.

The betel tree, facing him, kept on rocking madly; the tamal tree was endlessly wild. Lightening smote the thick veil of clouds. Then the wind dropped off and it seemed that any minute it might pour. Winding up the sails, the fishermen tried to steer their boats onto the shore. Their bodies couldn't take the weight of the loaded vessels but they managed, somehow, to push the pinnaces into the bog, pulling the oars unsuccessfully against the strong current of the Padma river, finally losing control, trying to navigate the rudder.

But the river embankment made such a show! A thin black line drew itself out all along the land at the edges of the river—then one heard splashes of the falling banks, one after the other—Padma ma was altering her course!

It was on a day like this one—when the surface of the river was in a state of turbulence—a river that flowed in his blood moved his bones—when a wild wind made a riot with tossed-up dust, and lent a mica-like shiny prospect to the scene—when the tamal tree continued to make a racket and the betel tree tossed and turned on the ground, that the two of them came and stood there facing each other.

The boy looked up and gazed at the face of the girl; he thought how perfect and vibrant the moment was—the ultimate gift of the generous river, its banks and the breeze that blew in. A unique moment, once captured never repeated—when the full current of life transcended the sorry measure of ordinary existence. The girl smiled, put her arms around him and gave him a kiss. "I have come braving the stormy night only for you," she said.

He hugged her tightly in his arms, then killed her by winding her own fragrant hair round her neck. 'Let me eternise this moment,' he thought. 'After this day, she too will become old; my life will be taken up by other occurrences, but this moment—which has no beginning or end—will never come again in this life. I can't allow its image to pale.'

He stared amazed at the girl. Outside, the tamal and the betel tree continued to create confusion. The river flowed indifferently according to her own mood. The wind dropped.

1968

The Divine Resonance

Jhankar

He had run away and come here, and was lost in meditation in the little but he had built for himself by the side of a stream in a dense forest at the pit of a mountain. His only thought was how to find the Saraswati Veena once again. All his mental exertions were directed to that one end.

Continually hurt trying to love his fellow human beings, he had tried to make it to a place in the world with the help of his intellect and alcohol. That was why society rejected him, his family abandoned him, his beloved wife deserted him, even his own children—the innocent, sublime creatures—cast him aside, and so he came to this forest and took refuge in this little hut, away from all human habitation.

Music was the sole object of his contemplation, but the Saraswati Veena that could transmit magic through music had already become extinct in this, our world. Nevertheless, he was hard at trying to make the instrument work—by fixing it, renovating it or completely overhauling it—nothing worked. He flung the instrument angrily to the ground—all at once it made a loud jingle.

It was a monsoon night. His mind was assailed by the modulations of the fourth in the major C scale. He was sitting, his face cupped in his hands, taking a sip of alcohol, from time to time. Suddenly the birds started warbling, as if from nowhere. He heard soulful music. Looking up he saw an extraordinarily beautiful woman standing in front of him. She had tender looks, was fair complexioned, dressed in immaculate white and atop a swan. She laughed and said, "You are my lover—come let's make love!"

How could this unbelievably beautiful woman, perfect in every way, appear in the forest deep, where the existence of the feminine was unthinkable? He thought it a matter to reflect on. Outside, the flashes of lightning suddenly vanished. The earth assumed a serene and quiet mood. The chirruping of the crickets grew faint and melted into the silence. The full moon of the month of *Magh* came up mysteriously and the four corners of the earth began to crumple up.

He got up and asked, "Who are you?"

"Take the Veena into your hands," she said, smiling softly.

He was in a state of shock. "Why it's the Saraswati Veena, that which had got lost—I was looking for it."

"Give it to me," she said.

He gave it to her.

The woman took up the instrument and strummed a euphonious tune. Just a twang—making him go to into a divine rapture.

It was the end of the world.

1968

Attack!

Maar

Arjun, in pursuit of Subhadra, made his appearance at the temple, in the city of Dwarka, after confabulating with SriKrishna.

At that moment, Subhadra, folding her two pure, fair palms, was immersed in the meditation of Brahma, the Supreme Being; she was surrounded by the illustrious clan of the Yadavas.

Ploughman Balaram was hard at work tilling the land—extracting nourishment from the bowels of Mother Earth. Srikrishna kept regarding him with a twinkle in his eye even as he imparted his mysterious message to charioteer Arjun to mount the steps of the shrine of Brahma.

Subhadra had, by that time, finished paying obeisance to the Lord and was bending and touching the feet of the deity. Suddenly, there was a mild knock at the door. Subhadra's female companions woke with a start. They immediately clamped their hands to Subhadra's pair of rosy, lotus-shaped ears and tried to keep the sound out of her hearing. But Subhadra had grasped the inner significance of the knock; she quickly got up and sat. She asked, "Who has knocked?" Her companions brushed the matter aside and said it was nothing, "Sounds like that are normal when the weather is foul."

Flaring the nostrils of her pointed nose, frowning deeply, Subhadra declared, "I know everything—don't tell me the untruth. He has come. I must go to him."

On his part, shaking his peacock-feathered crown, Srikrishna was telling Arjun, coming close, "My boy, restrain yourself." The eternal warrior, that was Arjun, reddened upto his ears. He gave one sharp pull at his bow. It sent the terrified Yadava clan scuttling like greedy vultures to Balaram, at the bosom of his ploughed field, to complain that Subhadra was about to be abducted.

In the meanwhile the door of the temple had come ajar. Subhadra almost swooned at the sight of Arjun's large petal-like eyes. She couldn't decide what she should do; her companions, lending her physical support, tried to bring her back to the citadel of Dwarka. But she had no strength to move.

Arjun commanded her to get up on the chariot. Srikrishna, the preserver of the equilibrium of the universe merely gave a brief smile. He did nothing to stop the Yadavas from launching an attack; they aimed their arrows at Arjun as soon as he lifted Subhadra into the chariot and moved ahead at great speed. Among the attackers, also in pursuit, was ploughman Balaram, law unto himself.

In today's parlance one could say that Srikrishna appeared wrily amused. Shafts had begun to fall on Arjun and Subhadra. She, the earth's foster mother—who belonged to none but the brave—exclaimed, "O Lord, O Charioteer, they are shooting at us—give me the reins of the chariot while you deal with them in whatever way you can."

Arjun made Subhadra in charge of both his serene and wild natured horses. Subhadra said, "I will direct the horses, you string your bow." What followed was unforgettable! The chariot rode up to the firmament of stars, with Subhadra at the helm and Arjun fighting a rearguard action. Finally gathering the entire Yadav clan, restoring harmony in their midst, Arjun, taking Subhadra along, celebrated his celestial wedding. We know about the history of their union from the records of Abhimanyu's entry into *Chakrabyuha*—a camp guarded by seven bands of armies. There is nothing in this world to compare with the story of their love! All along Srikrishna kept smiling naughtily, as was his wont—only ploughman Balaram was left fuming.

This is the way the world goes—especially in today's Bengal. Our previous generations were at an advantage as they managed their lives guided by the wisdom gleaned from our myths. We in this age, have lost the secret use of mythology in our lives.

What is left but to attack? Unless we fight we cannot solve any problem. Decadence has entered our souls, it is eating into our entrails like maggots. Those who are not reminded about Subhadra when they come across the half-starved housewife of number thirteen Nebutola lane are not men—not human beings at all. You might recall the comment of Sayed Wazed Ali—the same tradition continues.

Those who have the capacity to understand, would know, our India can survive forever only by scouring the images of our mythology. Our mothers and our sisters are the modern day Subhadras. Only those who can fathom the representativeness of these women would know the battle has not ended. Bengal has been torn apart because we have not articulated the wisdom of our ancient myths—for that, the fight is still ahead of us.

Yet—when I look around today's Bengal, I wonder where the Subhadra of yore might be found, where Arjun might abide, waiting to be discovered. But they must be, surely, existing here—of that I am certain, they are marking time to emerge as our progeny.

They have learnt how to come forth from the *Chakrabyuha* in their mother's womb like the mythical Abhimanyu.[1] Let them take up arms—the day has arrived when they must ready themselves for attack. The crimson coloured Shimul tree facing me, seems to be relaying a similar message.

1969

1. Abhimanyu was the son of Arjuna by Subhadra and in his courage the prototype of the new generation of revolutionaries. themselves for attack.

Acknowledgements

The translator gratefully acknowledges the affection, encouragement and help received from the family of Ritwik Ghatak—his wife Suroma and son Ritban—in translating his stories. Thanks are also due to Dr. Bikash Kumar Bhattacharya, Assistant Librarian, Sahitya Akademi Library, for identifying and locating the mythological sources of Ritwik's creative imagination; to Sumanta Banerjee for being the guiding spirit behind the volume; to Sonali Prakash for taking on the roles of reader, editor and critic and to Ira Bhaskar for allowing me to share her undiminished interest in Ghatak.